# Cargo

**Tom Gray**

1889 books

www.1889books.co.uk

ISBN: 978-1-9163622-4-6

*For Susan*

For Susan

# CARGO

CARGO

# ONE

It was in the run-up to Christmas and on a normal day, Vera's Cafe was usually at its busiest at eight in the morning. The three rows of four-seater wooden tables would be occupied and a selection of breakfasts would be being served. The place was warm and the atmosphere friendly; helped by the smell of sizzling bacon and fresh toast. Tony, who owned Vera's, had wanted to create a community feel, in order to attract locals as well as those passing through on the nearby Tube line. There were gingham table cloths and a selection of framed photographs on the walls of London scenes from the 1950s and 60s, including a signed photograph of some serious-looking young men called Reggie and Ronnie. Customers liked their food simple and cheap. It was the job of eighteen-year-old Adam Hicks and the other staff, to make sure that is what they got. Once the morning rush was over, there was an hour or so to prepare for the "brunch set," as they were called. These customers wanted coffee and such things as egg crumpet melts or quiche. Tony had added several vegan dishes to the brunch menu and these had proved to be popular and profitable.

Adam had worked for his uncle Tony, at Vera's, for a little over two years, having moved down to London from Sheffield, following the death of his mum. Not that Adam saw much of Tony. The daily management of Vera's was the responsibility of Tony's "man on the scene," Karol. It was Karol's job to do all the paperwork, sort out deliveries and bank the cash takings at the end of the day.

Just about the most important thing that Adam and the rest of the staff needed to remember, was to avoid going upstairs. Karol did not want his filing and storage systems to be touched by anyone. Upstairs was out of bounds, plain and simple.

Karol was usually friendly, and happy to share a joke with staff and customers. He was in his fifties, shaven- headed and with the physique of a man who, in the past, had spent a lot of time in a gym. Like one or two of the other employees, Karol was originally from Eastern Europe and had not quite managed to lose his accent. Karol's use of traditional London sayings were often the cause of much hilarity and Adam would mimic Karol's attempt to say: 'Hello me old china plates.' Regardless, Karol was still respected for his organisational skills and no one took liberties.

At 4.25, as Adam was cleaning up after closing time, the cafe door opened and to everyone's surprise, in walked Tony.

Tall, thin and with blonde curly hair, he loped around in a rather ungainly manner, like a giraffe with something on its mind. Despite this, Tony must have had a keen mind – always on the look-out for the next deal to do or the next business opportunity to consider. He flashed a cheeky smile at Adam before asking, 'Hey Adam, are you off up north after work tonight?'

'Yes, I'm off to good old Sheffield as soon as we're finished. I'm going back for a school reunion and to meet up with some old friends.'

'That's good. You and the others do a good job here. This place is a little gold mine. Did we sort that problem out with your wages?'

'Yes. Eventually.'

Tony pulled a wedge of notes from his pocket and, as he peeled some off, said: 'I'm sorry about that, mate. Here's twenty quid to buy some flowers for your mum's grave and another fifty for yourself, okay?'

'Thanks, Tony. Are you sure?'

'Don't be daft. You get going now and catch your train. I've got some stuff to sort out with Karol.'

Adam did not need to be asked again and was out of Vera's in double quick time, on his way to Sheffield.

# TWO

Adam looked at his phone and realised, with a sigh that there was still at least thirty minutes before he and his fellow passengers still left on the 17:58 from London St Pancras were due to arrive at Sheffield Midland Station. It was dark outside and, apart from staring at the sleeping man across from him, there was little else that Adam could think of to occupy his mind. He was having no second thoughts about attending the reunion at his old school, even if it had been two years since he had left with a few average grade GCSEs. Most of his friends at the Sir Arthur Edwards Academy had stayed on in the sixth form and would now be at university or in employment. Going back to school now, offered Adam the chance to show his face and remind some people that he had made something of his life. A levels weren't everything; besides which, his mum would have wanted him to make the effort to turn up, rather than hide away any longer.

Unwilling to pay for a taxi outside the station, Adam waited at a nearby bus stop and, as if welcoming him home, the Sheffield rain grew heavier and steadier. Several buses came and went before a number 41 arrived. Adam fought to stay awake as the bus splashed and squeaked its way southwards towards the Garner Estate. Adam's residence for the weekend was a flat on the fourteenth floor of Blunkett House. He knew that his arrival would cause problems, but, as far as he was concerned, it was worth it.

# THREE

Adam's last year at school had been a particularly bad one. His mother's condition was slowly worsening and she was regularly admitted into the Hallamshire Hospital, sometimes for as much as a week at a time. Adam's relationship with his step-father, Jeff, was growing worse and Louise, his sister, was almost never at home. She'd met a boy and spent most of her time at his house in Rotherham.

On one occasion, during one of his mum's hospital stays, Adam had arrived home from school and found Jeff asleep on the settee, clutching a half-empty bottle of whisky. The TV was on with the volume up too loud and most likely everyone in the tower block could hear Bradley Walsh sharing a joke with a contestant on some irritating game show. It was almost as if Jeff had been waiting for Adam to arrive because, within a couple of minutes, he was sitting up and complaining about how tough his life was and how Adam and his sister had not helped.

Before meeting Adam's mum, Jeff had divided his life between his job as a warehouseman in a factory and a selection of city-centre pubs. He'd been in trouble with the police from time to time, mainly for being drunk and causing a nuisance. Meeting Adam's mum had just about saved him from ending up being both homeless and hopeless. It had obviously been some time since Jeff had washed and perhaps even looked at himself in a mirror; over the preceding months, his haggard face had become buried under a grey beard, and an untidy ponytail trailed down his back. He was thin and despite a diet made up mainly of fried food and take-always he had not put on any excess weight. Years of heavy smoking had left his teeth stained and a walk up the stairs up to the flat was now a serious challenge, leaving him short of breath and, once back in the flat, frequently unable to walk again for some time.

'I'm bloody sick of you two lazy buggers. It's okay for you, swanning off to school every day and leaving me here to look after *your* mother. What's the point of Shakespeare and poetry anyway? Why don't you stop off for a day or two and do something around the flat, like cleaning or washing the bed sheets? And don't forget that it's *my* money that pays the rent and the bills. That uniform you've got on was paid for by me; yes me!'

Adam's commonsense told him not to be drawn into this discussion but the mention of his mother in Jeff's attack was too much.

'Excuse me,' said Adam, in an effort to seem like an adult, 'but this was our flat before you moved in. I do a lot for mum, in case you hadn't noticed. I take her out every day after school and I go to the shops. Don't forget that I go and fetch her prescription from the pharmacist, not you.'

Jeff had not expected Adam to stand up for himself like that. His rational response touched a nerve.

'You little… right, have some time to yourself then,' and with some speed, he leapt off the settee, grabbed Adam by the collar and, before he could react, Adam was being pushed through the door and out of the flat. His small frame crashed against the wall opposite and he slumped to the floor. Before going back inside, Jeff had stood over him and said, 'When you say sorry and when you start doing something useful, you can come back in. Until then, get lost!'

The door slammed shut and Adam was alone.

It was a wet afternoon and Adam was wearing only his school uniform and he did not have a coat or his phone. Picking himself up, he wandered about for a while hoping that someone might take pity on him and invite him to come in for a cup of tea or to watch TV. He had friends who lived in the same block and he knocked at their doors, but none seemed to be around.

Half an hour later, Adam decided that he may as well go for a walk in the woods that were adjacent to Blunkett House. He knew these woods well and, when they had a dog, he used to like taking it there, and would watch as it scampered and explored. He hoped that there might be a shelter, at least until the rain stopped. The heavy rain had made the usually placid stream that ran through the woods into something much angrier, and water was racing down. Adam stopped to get his bearings. If he jumped over here, then it would save him at least a ten-minute walk down to the wooden bridge. Besides which, Adam had crossed the stream at this point at least a thousand times and it was only a metre or so wide at this spot, even in its current swollen state. With a short run up, Adam leapt, but his foot slipped in mud as he took off and he tumbled head first into the water. Struggling to recover his senses, he gasped for air as the water rushed over him. He tried to lift himself up but his school bag had snagged on a jagged rock and he was unable to pull himself out or release himself from the bag with its strap across his chest. Thrashing and screaming, Adam felt desperation welling within him.

'Hold my hand,' a voice said from behind. 'I'll get your bag off that stone. That's it. Hold on to me and push yourself up.'

In seconds, Adam was back on his feet and out of the stream. As he wiped the water from his eyes, the person who had saved him came into focus. It was Lauren from his English class at school. She was looking at him with sympathetic eyes but clearly barely resisting the urge to burst out laughing. She lived on the "better" side of the estate, near the Catholic Church and the golf course, and was part of a group of girls who always seemed to look down on Adam and his friends. Typically, she was wearing what looked like an expensive raincoat, and beneath a wide-brimmed hat her blonde hair was neatly tied back in pig-tails. On her feet she wore pink Wellington boots with a flower pattern on the side, which, despite the weather, seemed untouched by any mud.

'Thank you, Lauren. I fell in.'

'That's pretty obvious; I didn't suppose you were having a swim.'

Adam thought he deserved this flash of sarcasm.

'What are you doing here anyway?'

Lauren's eyes looked down at the dog she was holding on a lead and realised there was no reason to answer his question.

'How about you? What are *you* doing in here?'

Adam tried to think of an excuse for being in the woods on a wet afternoon. 'I thought I'd get some fresh air.' He immediately wished that he'd been able to come up with something better.

'Well, I'd better let you get home to dry off. See you tomorrow. Don't forget that we've got that Macbeth homework to do for tomorrow.'

With that, Lauren and the dog took off around a bend in the footpath and were quickly out of sight. It was possible that Adam heard the sound of Lauren laughing loudly, though it may just have been water in his ears. Either way, he suspected that this incident would soon be common knowledge at school.

When Adam arrived back at the flat, the door was locked and Jeff was out. Having used his key to get in, he wrung out his uniform and put it over a radiator to dry. He then took a bath and went into his room, making sure to lock the door behind him.

# FOUR

Darkness has its uses and it prevented Adam having to look at the Garner Estate as the bus rattled through on its way to the terminus, opposite Blunkett House. "The Garner," as it was widely known, had once been the pride of the council, having been built to fit into the contours of a particularly steep valley on the edge of town. The 1960s architects and city planners had intended that living on the Garner Estate would be a fresh start for families who had been moved out of the run-down inner city areas and who they thought needed clean air, commanding views, dependable plumbing, inside toilets and gas central heating. Over the last twenty years, the Garner, with its concrete tower blocks and the accompanying maisonettes had become neglected and occupied by people with no sense of pride or respect for the estate. Council workers employed to repair the crumbling flats and roads, needed police protection from stone-throwing youths or those wanting to steal their vans and tools. Tonight, Adam was at least going to be spared the sight of the graffiti and litter – until the morning.

'Oh that's great!' A sign on the lift door read: LIFT OUT OF ORDER, and that meant a climb up the semi-lit stairwell to flat number 143.

As Adam approached the door of the flat, he could distinctly hear two voices coming from inside. He recognised one as Jeff's and the other was that of a woman. Adam turned the key in the lock and stepped in to the hallway. Facing him, with a surprised expression on his face was Jeff and, behind him, a woman was putting on a blue raincoat. She looked to be in her forties with close-cropped, dyed red hair and was heavily made-up. Jeff and the woman were preparing to leave the flat. Adam's unexpected arrival caught them both off-guard. For a very long moment, Jeff and Adam faced each other, both seemingly unable to find the words to match the situation. Jeff spoke first:

'Adam, what are you doing here?'

'I'm back for the weekend and, seeing as this is my family home, I'm staying here. What's your problem?'

'You don't live here any more. That's the problem. I said that we should have changed the lock, but she wouldn't have it!'

'No, you're wrong there. This was and still is mum's place and she said that I could always call it my home. Anyway, who's this?' Adam turned his head to look at the woman, who was by now starting to push herself closer to Jeff, as if she might need his protection.

'This is Cath and she lives here. *We* live here and, if you don't mind, we've got a taxi waiting, so off you go.'

Jeff took a step towards Adam and expected him to back away, but Adam stood his ground.

'Don't start! I can handle an old lad like you these days; I'm not a kid you can push around any more, so don't even think about it. I'm staying here for a couple of nights. You two go out and don't make a noise when you come back.'

The woman spoke and seemed aware of the potential for trouble in the situation.

'Jeff. Stop it. Leave him!' To Adam's surprise, she stepped out from behind Jeff and spoke directly to him. 'Hi, Adam. I'm really sorry Jeff didn't tell you I was moving in and didn't ask you if it was okay. It was

11

ages ago, but I was a friend of your mum's going way back. You used to go to school with my son: Luke Townsend. Remember him?'

Adam was too taken aback by her that the best he could do, in response, was to mumble something about Luke and offer a weak smile of recognition.

'It's fine to stay here, love, of course it is. Your mum would've wanted you to. Make yourself at home, love. Look, we've just got to go now. Come on, Jeff.'

With that they left. Jeff flashed a threatening look at Adam as he passed him.

Adam was alone and his thoughts turned to the many years living here with mum and Louise. Money was tight, but mum always found a way to give the kids what they needed. Jeff's arrival changed things and now Cath had stamped her mark on the flat. Mum's photograph had gone from the mantelpiece and in its place there was a picture of someone who Adam did not recognise. The furniture was different and the living room had been re-decorated. After a while, he made up the bed in his old bedroom and tried to settle down. There were no curtains in the room and a piercing arctic draught sliced through the rotting window frames. It had been a long day at work, and despite everything else, Adam was able to fall asleep very quickly.

# FIVE

The next day, Adam visited his mum's grave at the City Road Cemetery and laid some flowers next to the headstone. From the graveside Adam could see the city centre below him, nestling in the valley of the seven hills on which the city is built. Sheffield's suburbs stretched to the top of each of the hills. In the distance, one of the hills to the west had a TV mast on its summit, which he could just about see through the haze.

'I'm up here again mum,' he said to the plain granite headstone. 'You'll be glad to know that I'm still doing okay in London and I'm going to that reunion. They'll see that I've been able to start again, away from Jeff. What made you want to marry that bastard anyway? Sorry, mum.'

He promised her that he would return and set off back down the long flight of steps towards the cemetery gates and out into the noise of the living world.

Later that afternoon, having eaten a microwave meal and taken a bath, Adam walked the three miles up the steep hill to his former school. The reunion was set to start at 7.30, and as he arrived a number of friends and other familiar faces were gathering in the reception area. Sam Currie was the first to shake Adam's hand. Sam was always a well-meaning guy and had been Adam's closest friend during the hard times.

'How's tricks, Hicksy? What's it like down in London?'

Over the next hour, one school friend after another joined the growing crowds in the main hall. The buzz of chatter subsided long enough for a few speeches and presentations to be delivered before the sound of conversations started again.

'Fallen in any streams lately?' Lauren asked, during a break in conversation.

'Oh no! Lauren, I never thanked you for that. I must have looked so stupid!'

Rather than denying it, Lauren seemed to revel in reminding Adam of how pathetic he looked. 'I must say, that wasn't your finest hour. I remember that your bag was weighing you down and you were splashing about like a seal.'

'Really?' Adam tried to pretend he'd forgotten how cold and miserable he was.

'Anyway, you didn't drown.'

'Thanks to you.'

'Actually, after that, I decided to do some lifesaving training and I work part-time on a lifeboat now. I've saved twenty-three people from drowning in that stream this year.' Her eyes gave up the pretence at being serious and they both laughed.

'Didn't I hear that you've started at… don't tell me… The London School of Economics?'

'Yes, that's right. Well remembered'

'Can I have your number? We could meet for a coffee and I could show you around some of the places that are not on the tourist trail. I expect that you've been to all the usual places. That's if it's okay with you of course. I'm sure your boyfriend won't miss you for an hour or two.' Adam was glad to have slipped in the mention of a possible boyfriend, while hoping she'd tell him that she didn't have one.

'Oh, he's cool about me meeting guys for coffee. He's busy a lot of the time and, besides which, I'd love to be shown around London by a Londoner.'

'Great. Thanks.'

She wasn't "stick thin," like the other girls all seemed to wish they were, and that is one of the things Adam liked about her. She was, as his mum might say: a "bonny-looking lass." She had no airs or graces and he watched as she moved effortlessly between different groups of people and left them all with a smile.

And so the evening drifted on. Old friendships were revived and promises made to get together soon. Mr Tankard, the headteacher, was retiring after the next term and, in his usual way, he used this occasion to make a long speech about the value of education and how we should all respect each other. Just as everyone thought that he was just about to finish, he suddenly announced that he was going to award a special prize, to the person he considered had overcome the greatest difficulties in completing their education. Everyone stopped talking and looked around to see who this person might be. With a grand gesture, he announced:

'Ladies and gentlemen. Ali Hamza arrived in this country alone and with nothing. I won't repeat what he went through back home because you all know about it, but, despite that, he has never allowed this to stop him from making the most of every opportunity. He has exceeded what we ever hoped he might achieve and has a place at Sheffield University waiting for him, where he will study medicine. He is what this school is all about. Come forward Ali, and receive your prize.'

Ali shyly stepped forward and, with a huge round of applause, he held the silver plate in front of him. Everyone smiled and realised what odds this young man had overcome in his life. Somehow he had escaped those who trafficked him across the world and his smile lit up the room. For many, this was the highlight of the evening and they started to drift home. Having acquired Lauren's number, Adam walked down the hill with a satisfied smile.

Adam's second night in the family flat proved to be much more comfortable than the previous one. Before going to bed, Cath had put up some curtains in the bedroom and the bed now had a duvet and some clean pillows. There was a note for him on the kitchen table which read:

*Dear Adam,*

*Once again, I'm really sorry about how you had to find out about me living here. Had I known that you were coming, I would have made an effort to sort your room out and all that. Please don't get upset by Jeff. He really loved your mum and talks about her all the time. I get bored listening to him. lol. I understand that this flat has lots of happy memories.*

*Please help yourself to bread in the morning and if I don't see you tomorrow, I hope that you have a safe journey back to London. If you want to come up to stay again, let me know and I'll make up the bed etc.*

*Cath*

In the morning, Adam packed his possessions and within a couple of hours he was on a train back to London. Had he known what lay ahead, he might have taken more advantage of Cath's hospitality, but that would have involved spending more time with Jeff and that was not a good idea.

16

# SIX

As the train crawled its way towards London, Adam reflected on how his life had changed over the last two years, and he remembered his thoughts on that first journey down. Starting a new life in a strange town or city is rarely easy and Adam had expected there to be one or two problems along the way. He was not wrong.

Shortly before his mum died, Uncle Tony had promised her that he would take care of Adam and find him employment in London, as well as somewhere decent to live. On one occasion, Tony had offered to "fix" Adam up with one of the young women who worked for him, on a blind date. While it seemed a thoughtful offer, it was certainly too early for Adam to be planning his social life; he was scarcely an adult and was still grieving over the death of his mum. He knew that Tony owned several businesses and that there was a job waiting for him somewhere, but, even the day before, it had not been made clear exactly what work he would be required to do or where he would be living. Despite constant reassurances, Adam still worried.

Tony had arranged for a taxi to meet Adam at Victoria Coach Station and to take him to his new home, which was a flat on Oakington Manor Road, in Wembley. A neighbour would give Adam a key to the flat and he had the rest of the day to settle in, before being picked up in the morning, and taken to his new workplace.

To Adam's relief, the flat was clean, well equipped and relatively spacious. He knew in advance, that he would be sharing the flat with two of Tony's other employees, but neither of them was at home, so he found what he hoped was his bedroom and unpacked his belongings.

At just before six in the evening, Adam heard the door open and he found himself face to face with a man who he assumed was one of the other flatmates. The stranger was short, over-weight, in his mid-thirties with a receding hairline. He looked like he'd been working on a building site and was wearing mud-splattered clothing and heavy boots.

'Hi, I'm Jed. You must be Adam. Tony said that you would be moving in today. I see you've found your bedroom. That's good. There's no food in, as you've probably noticed, so I'm going around the corner to the chippy. Fancy anything?'

'I'd love some fish and chips.'

'Sure. Get some plates ready and I'll bring some back. I'll fill you in on what's what. See you in a bit.'

Later that evening, as Jed and Adam sat eating at the dining table, Jed completed some of the many gaps in Adam's knowledge about his new life and what to expect. Adam learned that the other occupant of the flat was a guy called Phil, who Tony employed as a driver and who was not there very often. By all accounts, Phil was a man of few words and preferred to play computer games or to stay at his girlfriend's house in Streatham. As he finished a can of lager, Jed said to Adam,

'Keep an eye on your pay packet. Tony's not the most reliable guy when it comes to your pay. Always check that you've been paid correctly. I'm okay because I work in my spare time as a DJ and that means that I can always get by.'

'Have you any idea where I'll be working or what I'll be doing?'

'Not really. Tony's got stuff going on everywhere. He's got beauty salons, properties that he rents out, cafes. He's even got a restaurant. I work on the property maintenance side, you know: doing up flats and making them fit to live in. This flat is one of twenty that he owns. The rent we pay is peanuts compared to most private landlords.'

Adam's eyes widened in horror at the mention of beauty parlours. 'What the hell would I do in a beauty parlour?'

Jed found Adam's expression particularly amusing and tried to reassure him.

'Don't worry. I'm sure that you'll be fine after a while. My guess is that you'll probably be working in one of the new cafes that he's opened. Even then, just make sure that you keep your head down, work hard and don't ask too many questions about money and stuff. Okay?'

'How did Uncle Tony make all this money anyway?'

'Ducking and diving. I'm off to bed now. See you tomorrow.'

# SEVEN

```
Hiya, fancy meeting up for a coffee sometime?
I'm free Saturday pm
Let me know
L xx
```

The text from Lauren had been sent at 11.30 a.m. and it was now 3.00 p.m.

```
Yeah great
```

Adam hesitated before adding anything else, for fear of sounding too keen. He must try to present himself as a man of the world, someone who is perfectly at home in the metropolis. Someone who is always meeting girls for coffee somewhere and might just be able to squeeze one more date into his already crowded social schedule.

```
What time?
Where?
I'm free most of the day
```

He thought that the last line about being free "most of the day" seemed just right, as it suggested that he might have something else to occupy his day. The truth was that he hadn't had much of a social life of late and that other than going to the cinema alone or occasionally to a pub with Jed, there wasn't much to it. Within 10 minutes, Lauren replied.

```
Good. I've been meaning to txt u
How about Saturday
Cozza Nova opp Kings X station
2pm ok?
Lxx
```

Between the exchange of text messages and Saturday, Adam got his washing and ironing up to date and by Friday night he had a selection of jeans and tee-shirts from which to select the ideal combination. Footwear was an easy one, given that he only owned two pairs of trainers and some sandals.

Saturday arrived and after a text from Lauren to confirm that he hadn't forgotten about their arrangement, Adam made his way across London to Cozza Nova.

When he arrived Lauren was waiting for him at a table by the window. She smiled and waved as they saw each other. Two hours passed as they talked about some of the teachers and the various memorable events of their school years. Adam spoke about growing up with a sick mother and an increasingly resentful step-dad. Lauren seemed interested and said that she would try to call in at Vera's when she could. Throughout it all, Adam tried to steer the conversation away from any mention of Lauren's boyfriend, but inevitably his existence came to the forefront of the conversation.

'So who is he then?'

'Who do you mean?'

'Your boyfriend.'

Much to Adam's disappointment, Lauren's boyfriend seemed to be exactly the opposite kind of person to himself. His name was Doug Randall and he was thirty, with a well-paid job in the financial world and a sports car. There was worse to come. Lauren told Adam that Doug had a flat in Clerkenwell and that they had been a couple, since he had approached her at a party, after which he had lavished her with just about everything she needed. Doug had booked a couple of

21

weeks off work in August and they were going to the Caribbean for a holiday. The real twist of the knife came when Lauren said: 'Hey, I've had a thought, why don't you come to Doug's place next Saturday? He's having a get-together and, when I told him that I was meeting you, he suggested that I invite you along. It'll just be a few of my friends and his mates. It'll be fun and I'd love you to come. You'll really like Doug.'

'Me? Really? Oh no, please, I'm terrible at parties and I usually end up in a scrap or getting on the wrong bus and having to walk eight miles home. I'm also the world's worst-dressed human being.'

'Don't be silly Adam. I want you to come. You might meet someone, you know, the love of your life! Some of my girlfriends from uni are coming and they're all lovely. '

She smiled and leaned across the table, her laser-like green eyes holding him motionless, like she'd been fitted out with some kind of secret weapon which rendered the victim temporarily unable to move a muscle. She pushed her hair back behind her ears and in a deliberately childish tone of voice whispered: 'Please Adam. For me?'

That proved the end of Adam's resistance and he grudgingly surrendered to her persuasive armoury. In truth, there was little that he wouldn't do if she asked him to do it.

'Right, that's a date then,' she said. 'I'll text you Doug's address. God, is that the time? I'm sorry, Adam, but I've got to dash. I'm supposed to be meeting Doug on Oxford Street at four and it'll take me ages to get over there on the Tube. He wants to buy me a new dress for next Saturday and I've also got some coursework to do.'

22

She leaned over, gave him a peck on the cheek and before he could say another word, she was gone. Adam was alone and lost in a world of disappointment that someone else was able to share her life and not him. Other people were looking over at his table and clearly wanted him to move, so, not wishing to stay any longer,  he left and started his journey back to Wembley.

What lay ahead was most probably a night alone in the flat. Jed had a gig somewhere and would most probably stay at someone's flat afterwards. Lauren's secret weapon had not yet released him, and during the journey home he remained trapped in her gaze and drugged by her perfume.

Back at the flat, Adam began to grow anxious about what he was going to wear to Doug's party and realised that any chance of impressing Lauren must start with improving his dress sense. He decided to go shopping the next day and fit himself out with some smarter clothes and shoes.

Later that evening, a song called "Out of my league" played in the radio and Adam felt instantly reminded of his place in the scheme of things.

# EIGHT

Adam was ten minutes early, when he reached the address Lauren had texted to him, so he decided to kill the time by walking to the end of the street and back again.

Seward Street itself was narrow with blocks of modern apartments built along either side. 'So this is where those people with posh jobs live is it?' he thought to himself. There was a small park at one end, with a sign at the entrance that said on it: "MAKING ISLINGTON GREENER, CLEANER AND SAFER."

No one was taking advantage of the opportunity for peace and quiet that this area seemed to offer, in fact there was nobody to be seen anywhere.

After several minutes of meandering along and back again, Adam decided that it was time to make an appearance at the party. His watch said 7.44, as he approached the address. Doug's flat was in a block that had a black metal fence running around and had four steps leading to the main entrance. Outside, to the left of the main door, was an intercom entry system, with occupant's name above a series of buttons:

FLAT 7

D.F Randall.

Adam pressed the buzzer and after a few seconds a male voice came through: 'Hello? Who is that?'

'It's Adam Hicks. I'm a friend of Lauren's.'

'Come in. We're on the second floor,' and with a "clunk" the front door opened.

Adam made his way up the stairs. A tall man, dressed in a dark suit and a white open necked shirt, was smiling warmly by the door with his hand out, ready for a handshake. He had dark hair, pushed back behind his ears and his tanned face was lit up by confident blue eyes.

'Hi. Welcome, Adam. Thanks for coming. I'm Doug. The drinks are over there, and please help yourself to whatever you want. Lauren's somewhere in there and you'll be pleased to know that she's been talking about you all day and hoping you would turn up. I've brought some caterers in and I've asked for the food to be ready to be served in about half an hour. So, until then, please relax get to know everyone.'

Adam stepped nervously inside and looked around. He could see smartly dressed people standing around, chatting in groups. No one took any notice of him as he stood alone, wondering what he should do.

The living room was open-plan and stylishly furnished, with an obviously expensive brown leather sofa against one wall and two matching armchairs facing it. On the far wall there was a large, mounted TV screen and, next to the window, on the right, a table generously stacked with wine other drinks. At the far end of the room there was a large and brightly lit dining area, with a wooden floor and tasteful kitchen units. Adam noticed Lauren in there, among a group of other young women. She was wearing a light blue summer dress and white sandals, her hair up in a neat bun. He thought she looked completely at home in this setting.

'Adam!' She rushed over and gave him a hug. 'Thanks for coming and I'm loving the suit and crisp white shirt. Is it by any chance new, and bought especially for tonight?'

He knew that it must be obvious to her that he had

tried really hard to smarten himself up and could feel himself blushing.

'Is it that obvious? he asked, feeling suddenly very self-conscious.

Lauren realised that she'd embarrassed him and tried to put him at ease. 'You look great Adam, I really mean it, and to think that you've broken the habit of a lifetime and come smartly dressed to see me!' She laughed with a freedom that turned heads.

Adam felt that he had to return the compliment. 'You look nice, anyway.' He wanted to say that she looked fantastic, but he managed to hold in the superlative.

'Thanks. I'm only a poor student you know. Most of the time I'm wearing jeans and a tatty sweatshirt and sitting in lecture theatres. I just happen to be going out with a bloke who wants to buy me posh clothes all the time. Oh, and he's also got this place! I sometimes wonder...' She paused and seemed somewhere else for a moment, before finding her train of thought: 'Anyway, Let's eat everyone!'

The guests were soon seated around a table and the caterers began to serve the food and drinks. Doug was at the head of the table, with Lauren to his left. The majority of the other guests were Doug's friends from work and their partners. Adam felt out of place from the start, as the conversation turned to what was going on at work.

'You know this business with Tim? Apparently, the Hong Kong office heard about it and called Vicky in the middle of the night and she had to go in to try and sort it out. Someone told me that Tim was in her office and getting it in the neck within two hours and – wait for it – that he came out crying! I love Vicky. Don't you think she seems much happier since the divorce?'

There was much laughter and agreement around the table, before someone added, 'Tim's such a turnip you know; you'd never guess he'd been to one of the better schools.'

'His mistake cost us thousands. Vicky says he'll have to pay it all back out of his commission. Serves him right!'

'Well, if they must hire posh boys who can't cut the mustard. I reckon Vicky will probably fire him anyway.'

More self- indulgent chuckles.

'Hey, Doug. You still driving that Porsche?'

Doug's eyes lit up at this. 'I certainly am. To be fair, it's a great car actually. Liam from accounts knows someone who knows someone who runs a Porsche dealership and I got it at a reasonable price. I love it.'

A plate of lobster on a bed of lettuce was placed in front of Adam, which immediately caused him to panic. He'd never even seen a lobster dish, let alone eaten one. He looked around to see how everyone else was eating it and tried to copy them, picking at it delicately. Though Adam thought he was eating with the maximum level of etiquette, he was unaware that his method was causing its own level of merriment among the other diners around the table. As far as he knew, he had not slurped, chomped or caused anyone to notice him, but he was wrong.

With the hint of a smile, Doug spoke from across the table, 'All right over there, Adam?'

'Yes thanks, this is lovely.'

'Good stuff! It doesn't matter how you eat it. Just get it down you.'

This was followed by a murmur of amusement around the table and one or two other comments quickly followed.

'Is that the Sheffield method then, Adam?'

'Hey! Watch it, I'm from up north too!' added Doug.

By now, Adam had finished and was trying to arrange the bit of shell neatly on his plate. Looking up, he noticed that everyone seemed to be looking at him and smiling. Lauren was the only one without a smile. She seemed concerned that Adam had become the centrepiece of the moment and, once again, tried to steer the focus away from his apparent lack of appropriate table manners.

'More wine, anybody?'

Her offer was taken up with enthusiasm and glasses were filled. Unfortunately for Adam, the addition of more alcohol merely added to the desire to scrutinise him. It did not take long before someone asked the question he'd dreaded answering all evening.

'What's your line of work, Adam?'

He had prepared himself for this and had decided to adopt a self-depreciating answer.

'I work in the food preparation and distribution sector,' he answered, and looked at Lauren for support. She smiled approvingly, until Doug put the boot in.

'You work in a cafe don't you, Adam?'

'Yes, I do.'

'What's it called?' someone asked. 'I might want a bacon sarnie one day.'

'Do you serve a range of teas? Assam? Nepalese? Oolong? Do you shop at Harrods? They do excellent bacon!'

'Do you need to reserve a table or do I just Google "grease" and hope I am able to get a table?'

By now, several people were unable to resist

laughing at the cafe-related jokes circulating around the table. It was only when the comments became personal that Adam began to feel the rage building inside him. The final strike to the bull's-eye of his patience came from Doug,

'I'm thinking of asking Vicky to hold this year's staff awards evening in Adam's cafe. Perhaps we could have a *Grease* theme. All the guys come as John Travolta and the girls as Olivia Newton-what's-her-name. Adam could come as one of the Chuckle Brothers, wearing a flat cap and stroking his pigeons?'

That was the end for Adam. He was no longer going to be the butt of any more jokes. Without a moment's hesitation, he threw the lobster that he was holding across the table at Doug. The flying lobster smashed into several bottles, sending their contents swishing over the table. Some of the girls – and men – screamed as Adam hurled whatever he could find at Doug. Having charged his way over to where Doug had been sitting, Adam grabbed him by the throat and snarled: 'You lot can shove your posh bleeding food up your arse. As for you, I'm gunna mash your face to a pulp!'

Pretty soon, the kitchen became a whirlpool of flying fists and bodies falling over each other. Adam's anger seemed to double his determination to punch Doug and as many of his friends as he could.

This saloon brawl scene lasted for no longer than two minutes, but Doug's kitchen resembled the scene of a bloody battle and eventually, with a threat to hammer anyone who dared to follow him, Adam stormed out of the flat to go home. It was only when he was half way there, that he realised how his behaviour would have affected Lauren and even worse that he had destroyed whatever chance that he had of ever have of taking her away from Doug.

# NINE

Over the next two weeks, the events at Doug's place played on Adam's mind. The sensible thing to do would have been to call Lauren and apologise for his behaviour, but the memory of the taunting from Doug and the others, was so painful that he could not find it in himself to apologise.

The fact remained, however, that he was bored and lonely. Lauren had not called or messaged him. He needed something else. He needed someone else to be with, someone with whom he could share his day-to-day moans and groans. He wanted a girlfriend, but getting anywhere near anyone who might be interested was limited by the long hours he worked and the absence of any opportunity to go out and be in the right place to do so. As much as he had baulked at Tony's offer of arranging a date with someone, the offer began to grow more attractive as his loneliness grew stronger. It was time to move on from Lauren and asking Tony to set something up seemed like the only option.

Hi. Sorry to be a pain but is that offer of meeting up with someone you know still on?

Tony's reply arrived within five minutes.

Heyup mate. Yeah I'll sort something out. Katie thinks that some girls at one of the salons need a night on the town. She's a slave driver LOL. I'll ask her to see if any of them fancy a blind date with a hunk LOL. Give us a coupla days. T

Adam felt relieved to have finally made the move. He was not interested in any kind of serious relationship, he just needed to be with someone new and perhaps even someone who might be remotely interesting.

Tony was true to his word and when Adam woke on Monday morning, there was a message from him. It had been sent at 3.00 a.m.

Mate. Sorted you out with one of the girls. Katie says she's really pretty and all that and fancies a night out. Promise me you'll behave like a gentleman LOL.
Think that the best thing is you two come out with K and me as a foursome and then you two can go somewhere after if you want. Her name is Helia. Her English is ok. Don't do owt daft cos she's got some big brothers LOL. I'll text you later with time and place.

So that was it. The Lauren era was over and Adam had something to look forward to, with the possibility of some happier times.

# TEN

Tony's text arrived, like the other one, in the early hours of the morning.

```
Mate.
Meet you at Wilders on Egan Street. Saturday 7:30
Smarten up it's POSH!! T
```

Google Street View revealed Egan Street to be in the heart of the West End. Tony wasn't messing about! Adam's immediate concern was that he might have to put some money towards the bill, which would certainly be enormous. His salary was more than reasonable for a cafe worker, but would not stretch to Tony's level of evening expenditure. It was too late to back down and so, on Saturday, early as usual, Adam found himself looking through the window of Wilders and trying to avoid thinking about the price of the dishes being consumed by those already enjoying their meals.

The wait was not long and a white Maserati, with Tony behind the wheel, pulled up next to him and parked right outside the restaurant. Tony was quickly out and opening the passenger door for Katie and a young woman to get out of the back. The front passenger seat was occupied by a large, smartly-dressed man who then moved into the driver's seat and, after a brief conversation with Tony, drove off.

'Hi, Adam. You know Katie don't you? Course you do. Anyway this is Helia.'

A tall young woman, barely old enough to be called a woman in truth, was standing shyly and was clearly unsure what to do or say. Adam thought she looked as if she might be from the Middle East. She had long, shiny black hair, brushed over to one side and had large brown eyes. She smiled shyly and held out her hand and Adam did the same.

'Hello, Adam. My name is Helia.'

She was wearing a dark dress, red shoes and carried a gold clutch bag. Adam noticed how she moved as they made their way to a table. She held her head high and her walk had an economy of effort, like a swan gliding across a lake. He hoped that her company would be as enjoyable as her obvious grace and beauty.

Wilder's was bustling with energy and there were very few spare tables, but at the sight of Tony and his guests, the Maître d' was quickly across and directed them to a table on a elevated level, overlooking the main dining area, in its own private space, Immaculately attired staff hovered around, looking to meet the needs of the customers. Tony's table had its own designated team of staff, who fussed around the four guests and had plainly been charged with ensuring that they gave the very best service to those at this table.

Not surprisingly, the food and service were far beyond anything that Adam had ever experienced. Helia seemed to enjoy the conversation around the table and certainly, in the subdued light of the restaurant, she appeared reasonably relaxed.

'So you are Tony's family?' she asked.

'Yes, my mum was his sister and after she died, Tony asked me to work for him.'

'Ah, I see, but you are not from London?'

'No, I'm from Sheffield.'

'Shefy... Shef... How do you say that? Where is

34

that?'

'It's Sheffield, with a *field*.'

'Ah.' She had another attempt to say the name, before starting to giggle at her own inability to get it right.

Adam thought her laughter was charming and was glad that, at last, she felt able to talk to him.

'It's about two hundred kilometres north of London. To be honest, there's not much there for me now.'

'I'm sorry. No family?'

'Not now. Now my mum has gone; I think I'll stay in London now. What about you? Where do you come from?' He noticed that she looked in Katie's direction before answering, as if she might need approval for her answer.

'I'm from...' Oddly, she hesitated as if trying to remember where she came from. '...Tromso, which is in Norway. Yes, Tromso. It's a very nice town.'

'So how come you live in London now?' Once again, Adam noticed how she looked towards Katie, deep in conversation with Tony and unaware of what was being discussed.

'There aren't any really good jobs in Tromso and I wanted to see new places, so here I am.'

'I see. Do you miss home?'

'Yes, of course, but I like it here and I'll probably go home sometime later in this year. I'm so lucky to have my job with Katie and she looks after me and the other girls very well.'

Almost as soon as Helia said this, both Tony and Katie halted their own conversation and looked across at her, seemingly interested in what she might say next.

Adam got the impression that they thought she

shouldn't have mentioned any other girls, although he saw particularly nothing strange about such a remark.

Tony was quick to change the subject.

'Right, who wants to order some more drinks? Adam? Go on, be a man and have a brandy with me. Helia, love, have a gin and tonic with Katie. That's a proper girl's drink. Us real men like our brandy after a good dinner, eh, Adam?'

Before Adam had a chance to say anything else, Tony snapped his fingers to place his order.

The drinks kept coming until around 10.30 when Tony glanced at his phone and asked to be excused for a moment.

'Sorry about this, everyone. I've got to make a call. Something's come up, business-wise. I'll only be a minute.'

'Oh, Tone! You said no business tonight. Can't it wait?'

Kissing her lightly on her forehead, Tony added, 'I'm sorry, my little Pooky, but Karol wants a word about... some deliveries that we need. Stuff for the houses and that. I'll be outside... but a moment.'

Katie seemed to accept the explanation before excusing herself, leaving Adam and Helia alone. For a moment Adam wondered if this was a deliberate move on their part to leave the two young people alone, in the hope that their relationship might blossom and that the seeds of romance may be sown. Again, it was Helia who started the conversation.

'Adam, you seem like a nice guy. Yes?' This seemed to come from nowhere and took Adam very much by surprise.

'Well... erm... I try to be.'

'How well do you know Tony?'

'He's my uncle. Mum's brother. He's my boss… '

'Yes, I know that, but do you know about his business?'

Adam was fumbling for anything meaningful to say.

'He owns Vera's and my flat and some other things. Katie sorts out the salons and the female stuff.' He was aware that all of this sounded very naive and simply stated, but it was really the limit of his knowledge, after all, he had never been asked to list Tony's businesses in such a way.

'I have to trust you. Take this and don't read it until you are alone. Please don't say anything to Tony. Okay?' She then, under the table, passed him a tightly folded scrap of paper and pushed into his hand. Without any hesitation, Adam took it from her and slipped it into his trouser pocket.

'What is this anyway?'

'Shut up, she's coming. Please read and trust nobody.'

Katie was by now only a couple of metres away from rejoining them at the table and Helia threw her head back and began to laugh as if Adam had said something amusing. In a show of affection, she then rested her head on his shoulder.

'Oh, I'm so glad you two are getting on so well. I knew you would. Tony asked me to find the perfect girl to bring and it looks like I was right.'

By now Adam was thoroughly confused, both by the mysterious note and Helia's show of affection, but he pretended to be happy that he had made her laugh and to add to the charade he gently brushed her hair away from across her eyes.

'Listen, I'm really sorry, Helia, but one of the kids has got a temperature and Tony and I have got to go.

I'd leave you with this fine gentleman,' she said, looking at Adam, 'but we're your taxi, aren't we? You'll have to come with us. Don't worry about the bill, it's our pleasure.'

Without questioning Katie's decision, Helia put on her coat and turned to face Adam.

'It's been very nice meeting you Adam.'

'Yes, you too. Take care.' Adam was slightly bemused at how quickly the evening had come to an end.

He would have liked to spend more time with Helia and he wanted to ask for her number, but all he could do was to follow her outside and watch as she climbed into the Maserati and was driven away. As they left, he could see Katie and Helia were already engaged in a serious conversation about something. He got the impression that Katie was annoyed by something and that Helia seemed to be bearing the brunt of Katie's anger.

It was late in the evening and Adam fumbled about in his pocket for his Oyster card. But instead he pulled out the piece of paper that Helia had given him. As he toyed with the idea of reading it he became aware of someone standing nearby and, sure enough, a man was standing in the restaurant doorway looking at him. The shape of the man seemed familiar, although in the half-light and after so much brandy, Adam found it hard to focus on the figure in much detail. For a moment the figure and Adam stood looking at each other until eventually the man made his move and, as he grew closer, Adam recognised him. It was Karol.

'Hey, Adam. How are you?'

'Hi, Karol. What are you doing here?'

'Minding my own businesses.' Karol's usual

joviality was missing and he now seemed large and unfriendly. 'You have a nice time with Uncle Tony and the girl, yes?'

'Yes, it was nice. Lovely food.'

'That's good. Now you go home safely my friend and you can tell me more at Vera's on Monday.'

With that Karol turned and melted into the crowds of people who were milling down Egan Street in search of food, drink and entertainment.

Strangely, though, as he walked to the Tube station, and even when he was on the train, Adam sensed he was being followed and several times he had to resist the temptation to turn around and see if indeed anyone was behind him.

The train home was filled with noisy late night revellers who posed no threat to anyone except themselves. Yet that awful feeling of being watched would not go away. As he walked the last half-mile from the station to his home, Adam felt certain someone was behind him, occupying the shadows. He ran the last few yards, holding the door key out in front of him, so that he could get it in the lock and escape the attention of whoever it was. Adam slammed the door and rammed the bolt across and firmly into place. As he stood inside, leaning against the door, he was sure he could hear someone breathing heavily outside on the landing and that a voice was whispering in a language other than English.

Half an hour later, and after a cup of tea, Adam had just flopped into bed, when he remembered the note from Helia. It was still in his trouser pocket, but his clothes were by now scattered across the floor, and besides his head was spinning from the brandy.

'It'll wait until morning.'

What was written on the scrap of paper was to put Adam in more danger than he had ever known.

# ELEVEN

It was as well that it was Sunday morning and Adam had time to recover from the night before. He opened his eyes for the first time at eleven, but it was just before midday before he was able to find the energy to climb out of bed. He knew that he should read Helia's note, but the desire for tea and toast was too great and so decided that it could wait. Maybe he had the prospect of meeting her again – assuming that she had given him her number. If she was interested, he decided that he'd play it cool and wait a couple of days before calling, just to keep her hanging on.

Before throwing the clothes that he had worn on the previous evening into the washing machine he took out the note and read it. On it was written:

*Please help us. We have come for work, but they keep us here. We all pay for journey and for work. We hear engines of planes all the time and the window shakes. We work for no money or begging. There are children with us. You not tell Tony or other men or they kill us. Marco died in the truck and they left him. They move us to other houses.*

This was not what he had expected to read. He knew that something was strange about her, but he had not sensed that Helia might be in any kind of trouble or unable to say what she wanted. Who was she? What were Tony and Katie doing when they brought her to meet him? Was this just one of Tony's practical jokes? This note was apparently a desperate cry for help and intended for someone with the ability to do something about it, rather than someone like him. Was Tony responsible for whatever was being done to these people? Now that Adam knew about it, where did that leave him? Did it make him a criminal if he did not try to help or tell the police? There was also his own position to consider. Without Tony's support Adam had nothing.

For much of the day Adam paced around the flat and tried to work out a way to deal with this new information. What he needed was to have someone to share this with, but deciding who to trust was another problem. Jed might listen, but it was unfair to burden him with all this. After all, Jed needed work as much as he did. Adam had experienced loneliness before, but this was on a new level. In the end he decided that the best thing was to tell no one and carry on as normal, then try to find out more about what was going on. Without any evidence the police would probably tell him to get lost and then what?

# TWELVE

It had been a particularly busy Wednesday, when Adam turned over the sign on the door, so that it said "closed." He would have preferred it, if it had read: "No more bacon until tomorrow, so go home and get a life!"

Karol had cashed up and then gone to a wholesaler to buy some supplies. It was 5.30 and time to start the journey home.

Apart from some pushing and shoving, it was an uneventful journey home, until the train arrived at Kilburn Park station. It was then that Adam realised that his phone was missing. Trying not to look too disturbed, he went through his pockets, before remembering he had put the phone down next to the till and that he must have forgotten to pick it up before leaving. At least that's where he hoped that he had left it.

With a sigh Adam got off the train and set off back to Vera's. It was close to 7.00, when he arrived back at the cafe. As he turned the key in the lock he noticed that, while the blinds were closed and the ground floor of the cafe was dark, some lights were on in the upstairs rooms. The main door was locked and so whoever it was up there had locked it behind them. Adam knew that all he should do was to find his phone and leave as quickly as possible, but he felt compelled to see who was up there.

As he crept silently towards the stairs, he heard voices coming down towards him. They were not speaking English and were angry about something. Instinctively, instead of simply explaining why he was there, Adam decided to hide. He crouched down and crawled behind the counter, hoping not to be seen or heard. In seconds, two men were downstairs and standing on the other side of the counter, only a short distance from where he was kneeling. Time decided to take a break and stand still for a while, as the disagreement between the men became louder and more aggressive in tone. Adam felt cramp growing in the back of his right leg but the fear of being caught stopped him from moving a centimetre.

After what seemed like days the conversation became more amiable. Whatever the disagreement had been about seemed to have been resolved. The men had moved away from the counter area and were now sitting face to face at one of the tables closest to the window, allowing him to stretch his legs a little and look around the corner of the counter to see who these people were. Despite the cafe being in semi-darkness and the only light coming through the blinds from the streetlights outside, carefully Adam peered around the bottom corner of the counter. What he saw did not lift his spirits at all, nor did it raise his hopes of getting out in one piece.

Perhaps it was the gloom or the tension of the situation that had made Adam unable to recognise Karol's voice as one of the two men at the table, or possibly that Karol was speaking in his native language. In any event, it was definitely Karol sitting there. As usual he was wearing his weather-beaten brown leather jacket, blue jeans and grubby trainers. He was looking intently across the table at the other man, as if waiting for the reply to an urgent question. Karol's companion seemed older, with long grey hair. On the table between the two men there was something that looked very much like a revolver and, as he spoke, Karol's companion repeatedly picked it up to toy with it. As they talked both men made a point of looking at their phones for messages and were frequently checking their watches. It was clear that they were waiting for someone to arrive and their wait came to a sudden end with a loud knock on the window.

On another occasion it might have been amusing to see two men leap out of their seats and let out cries of alarm, but not this time. Purposefully, Karol moved towards the window and pushed the blinds apart to see who it was. Adam could see the shape of a person on the other side and a vehicle parked outside, with its lights on and engine running. With a gesture indicating some degree of anxiety Karol indicated that the third man should go around the back of the cafe and come in through the back door. After pocketing the gun, the older man moved back towards the counter, with Adam still crouching there, before going through the kitchen and opening the rear door to speak to the new arrival.

What was spoken next was in English and Adam realised immediately, even without being able to see him clearly, that the visitor was Phil. His west-country accent was unmistakable.

'Where have you been?' growled Karol.

'Don't start on me. The coppers are all over the place, closing roads off and all sorts. We had to stop for a bit and lay low until they'd gone.'

'Better late than never. How many have you got?'

'Thirteen. I found one kid was dead and had to dump him in a skip near Ashford. Let's get 'em in. I was supposed to be back in Dover an hour ago and

45

Tony will be going mad. You know what he's like.'

'To hell with him, we're the ones taking the risk. Come on then, hurry up. Get them out of the van and send them through to us and we'll get them upstairs. Move it!'

Adam could hear orders being given, followed by what sounded like the sliding doors of a vehicle and then, silently but steadily, he could see the shapes of people coming inside and being hurried, sometimes pushed forcefully by Karol, up the staircase. They were so close to Adam that he could have reached out and touched their feet.

He counted seven adults, both male and female, and the legs of several children, shuffling past in the semi-darkness. All were absolutely silent as they came inside and upstairs. The whole parade lasted no longer than a minute or two before the rear door closed, an engine started and the van began to reverse back down the narrow alley and out on to the road.

Adam's luck changed when the long-haired man went upstairs, pushing the last of the visitors upstairs and using threatening language as he did so. After picking up his phone Adam saw his chance to escape from the counter, so he silently slipped out and locked the door behind him.

# THIRTEEN

The following morning, when Adam arrived at Vera's, the door was already open and Karol and one of the other employees, Kristoff, were sitting at a table drinking coffee. They were deep in conversation and it was a minute or two before either of them noticed that Adam had come in and had started wiping down the tables around them and preparing for the day ahead.

Karol was the first to see him. 'Good morning Adam, my young friend,' he said. 'How are you today? Keeping out of Barney Rubbles with the ladies?'

'I'm good Karol. You?' Adam replied, trying not to show any amusement.

'Oh yes, I just get on with things you know. Busy, busy that's me!' Karol broke into a broad smile and laughed loudly, as if he thought he had said something entertaining. 'Now I must go out and I think I'll be out for most of the day. Have a good day, my merry men, and I'll try to get back as soon as possible. Byes.'

'Bye.' Adam replied with a smile as Karol's thick-set frame disappeared briskly out through the door and into the street.

The rest of the morning slid by without any incident. The only moment out of the ordinary was when an elderly man, having eaten a full English breakfast, discovered that he had left home without any money. The policy at Vera's was to take his details and trust that he will return to pay. Kristoff was all for frog-marching the old man home and insisting that he must hand over the cash "or else." Adam, despite being so much younger and less experienced in these matters, said that they should trust the man to return with payment. Much to his relief that was the case, and the old man returned and paid his bill.

Adam allowed himself a satisfied smile after the last of the "breakfast mob" had finished and left. Kristoff was busy loading the dishwasher and they knew that they would have a quiet hour or so before the brunch customers arrived.

Adam sensed that after the events of the previous night, he had to take his chance to go upstairs and satisfy his curiosity, but in order to do that, he needed an excuse. The only thing that they were remotely short of was paper roll for the till, on which receipts are printed. He had hidden the spare roll in order to give the impression that there would soon be a shortage. Kristoff had not noticed this problem and seemed alarmed that someone might have to go upstairs. Adam played his part with aplomb.

'Kristoff, what are we going to do? We need that till roll very soon. Where's bloody Karol when you need him? I'll just have to go up there and look for some.'

'No, man. Don't even think about it! You know we can't go up there. Can't we manage with what we've got left?'

'Definitely not. I'll give him five more minutes then I've got to go up and find it.'

'Oh please, Addy. Give it ten!' There was now more than a hint of panic in Kristoff's voice.

Ten minutes came and went. One or two "brunchers" had arrived and were enthusiastically looking at the menu before ordering.

'Look, we're in charge here and we can't wait any longer, so I'm going up. I'll only be a minute,' said Adam.

He reached the landing and was faced by three doors- all closed. Inside one of these was what he supposedly needed. He decided to try the door nearest the top of the stairs and entered, his heart pounding. It was an office. The first thing he noticed was that there were several maps on the walls. Geography had never been his strength, but he recognised them as maps of Europe and South-East Asia. In front of the window, there was a desk, complete with PC and monitor. On top of the desk, next to the phone was a stack of papers, some passports, a calculator and a few pens in a mug. Adam could not resist the urge to walk the few steps towards the desk and have a closer look. On the top of the pile of papers was a Eurostar timetable, with departure and arrival times highlighted in yellow. One or two hand-written comments were scribbled on it. Beneath that, was a list of addresses in the London area, with scrawled annotations. Adam's suspicions were aroused and he thought that it might be helpful if he took one or two photographs to look at when he had time. A key had been left in the lock of one of the drawers. 'What harm would it cause to peek inside?' he thought, and so, with a slightly shaky hand, he turned the key and gently opened the drawer.

Lying there, black and cold, was a revolver and, still gently rolling around, some bullets. Next to them was a roll of bank notes, held together with a rubber band. Immediately alarm bells rang in Adam's head and with haste the desk drawer was locked again and he headed towards the office door.

He still had to find the storeroom. Logically, the next door to try was the middle of the three doors and Adam stepped into it.

It was a largely empty room, perhaps five metres

square. Scattered about the floor were adult and children's clothes, shoes, boots and what looked like documents. Here and there were half-empty bottles of water, empty sandwich cartons and crisp packets. It looked like the people who arrived last night might have been taken in there before being given something to eat and then moved on again. Adam's thoughts were jolted back by the sound of a voice at the bottom of the stairs. It was Karol.

'Hey Kristoff. Is everything okay here? I got stuck in traffics and couldn't get here any sooner. Where's Adam?'

'Adam? Er… he had to just go out for a minute,' answered Kristoff. 'He's gone after someone who left his wallet on the table. He'll be back in a minute. The bloke's only just gone out.'

Karol seemed satisfied with the explanation, though perhaps only because no one was waiting to be served and Kristoff seemed to be on top of things while Adam was supposedly out.

'Anyways, I'm going upstairs to do some work. Call me down if you need me.'

Adam looked for somewhere to hide, his heart exploding through his chest. The idea of Karol finding him up there, even on an innocent mission to find a paper roll, brought sweat to his forehead and brittleness to his knees. He imagined being tied to a chair and made to confess to being a spy. His breath seemed not to want to leave his body, for fear of being overheard. It was Kristoff, who came to his rescue.

'Hey Karol, before you go up, can I show you something that's worrying me in the kitchen?'

'Sure. What is it?'

'I think the dishwasher is leaking. Come with me

and I'll show you where. I don't want to keep you from your work, but I really feel you should take a look.'

'Of course. Let's go and have a looks.'

Adam could hear Kristoff and Karol walking into the kitchen, this was his chance to get downstairs. He can only have made physical contact with two of the stairs, such was his eagerness to get down them. His brain was working at such a level of self-defence, that he hurried into the cafe area and, without hesitation, began taking payment from a customer at the counter.

'That's... eleven pounds and sixty-three pence please sir... Yes, we accept that card. Place your card there and hold it for a second... there you are. Here's your receipt. Thank you very much... please call again. Bye!'

Adam tried to project his voice so that Karol would realise he was back and working. The idea worked and soon Karol appeared at his side behind the counter.

'Hey, Adam. Did you find the man and give him his wallet?'

'Yes. The poor man's got something up with him and is always leaving something behind. Oh, by the way, we're nearly out of paper roll for the cash register.'

'Okay, I see. I should have got back sooners, but I was delayed. We've got some upstairs and I'll go and get some. Hang on.' Within a minute or two, Karol was back with a roll of paper and the afternoon at Vera's resumed its usual pattern.

Karol went back upstairs and the two young men, apart from exchanging occasional glances, said nothing about what had happened.

Soon it was closing time and once the last of the customers had left, Karol emptied the cash register and was checking through the receipts. With a smile, he wished Adam and Kristoff "goodnights" and asked them to turn off the main light and lock the door behind them. Adam was keen to get away and as far from Vera's as he could. Before he could turn in the direction of the Tube station, Kristoff pulled at his sleeve.

'So what did you see up there?'

Adam recalled the sense of terror he had experienced earlier and it seemed too much to go through that again.

'Let me have a night to take it all in and I'll tell you more tomorrow. I'm a bit knackered now. Thanks for making that stuff up about the dishwasher.'

Kristoff began to laugh. 'Bloody hell, I had to think on my feet then, I'll tell you!'

'You saved my kneecaps. He'd have killed me,' said Adam seriously.

'It's okay, but you owe me one now. Agreed?'

'Definitely. Cheers again, pal! See you tomorrow.'

With that, Kristoff hurried off in search of a bus to his home, south of the river. The sight of that gun, those bullets, and all that abandoned clothing was still fresh in Adam's memory. One thing seemed certain to him was that something terrible was going on and that Vera's was at the heart of it.

# FOURTEEN

The flat was empty when Adam arrived. The sink was full of dirty plates and dishes and there was no milk in the fridge. He found a can of lemonade in a cupboard and slumped on the settee, trying to calm his nerves. What he needed was someone to talk to and help him make some sense of things and an hour later, his wishes were granted when Jed returned with a carrier bag full of groceries.

'Hi, Adam. You were late home, so I went to buy some stuff to eat. You look like crap. What's up?'

'I'm glad to see you, mate. Make us a cuppa and I'll tell you.'

'Sounds heavy. Give us ten and I'll bring it in.'

'Cheers, Jed. I'm going nowhere.'

A few minutes later, Jed appeared with a steaming mug of tea and a plate of pasta. Adam began to tell him about what had taken place earlier at Vera's.

Jed's face grew pale and increasingly serious as he listened to Adam's account of events.

'Are you sure that it was Phil?' he asked.

'Bloody positive,' answered Adam. 'And for God's sake, don't say a word to him.'

'Listen, Adam. I want you to take some advice from me, okay?' There was a sudden change in Jed's face and, for a short time he seemed to almost have taken on another personality. He moved close to Adam and spoke in a whisper.

'You're obviously getting a bit too close to something much, much bigger and more dangerous than you can handle. Back off. Just get on with your job and your life. Whatever you do, don't tell anyone else about what you've seen. Get it?'

Adam was alarmed by Jed's sudden intensity and wished that he hadn't mentioned anything to him. Jed gripped Adam's arm.

'And another thing. Do not try to be the hero or tell the police. Those guys will take you out in no time and nobody gives a damn about you. You're a nobody. Do you want to end up, in a bloody skip, with no face?'

Adam struggled to free himself from Jed's hold, but, like an animal caught in barbed wire, there was no escape. 'Okay, Jed. Let me go now, I get it.'

'Make sure you have.'

Later in the evening, when alone, Adam wondered if he was wise to have trusted his flat-mate with his secret. If it was not wise, then he might have made his biggest mistake.

# FIFTEEN

Adam needed a holiday. He had done so many weeks at the cafe, without talking a break that he was due at least ten days off, and, so, after a call to Tony's office it was arranged that from the following Monday someone else would be sent over from another cafe to cover him for a week. Tony's employees were only ever allowed a week off at any one time.

On his way home from work, that evening, Adam checked his phone for messages or missed calls. There was just the one voice message. It was from Lauren. Nervously, he pressed the code to listen to it.

*Hi Adam. Sorry I haven't been in touch, but there's been a lot going on and... well I didn't want to bother you. Please will you give me a call soon. I need to talk to you. Bye.*

Just hearing her voice, reminded Adam of why he'd fallen for her in the first place. He felt a wave of sorrow at having lost touch for a while, but, at the same time, the memory of being mocked by those people was still a source of anger. Lauren, it seemed to him, had taken Doug's side. She'd been happy to rush across town to meet Doug and allow him to buy her dresses or to spoil her in other ways, while Adam was locked into a life of working in a cafe without much hope of escape. He knew he should call her but it took several hours of pacing around until he decided that he needed her friendship, however much she's upset him.

He called at eight and she was quick to answer,
'Hi, Lauren. I got your message. Are you okay?'
'Fine. I'm glad you called back. I thought you might

55

not want to. It took me days to get all that bloody tomato sauce out of my hair after you trashed Doug's party. What are you, eh? You daft sod!'

'I know, but I sort of lost my temper…'

'Sort of? Sort of? I thought that you were going to thump everyone there… including me!'

'I wouldn't ever do that. So how did Doug take it?'

'Oh, he was made up about having his flat coated in blood and lobster. In fact he wants to invite you back, so that you can finish the job and ruin all the other rooms.' It was obvious that Lauren had retained her ability to use sarcasm as a deadly weapon.

'Is that why you called? Has he asked you to get some money from me to pay for the damage?'

'No, Adam. In fact I'm not with Doug any more. It's over.'

There was no point his pretending otherwise. Adam was delighted to hear that Lauren was free again and without any hesitation he asked: 'Can we meet up again? I've missed you, if you know what I mean. Please don't take that the wrong way, it's just that you're a friend and…'

'Yes please. Her enthusiasm caught him pleasantly by surprise. I'd love to catch up with you. It's been far too long and so much has happened. Adam, I need a friend.'

'That makes two of us. How about if you come over for a meal one evening?'

'Bacon and eggs, fried tomatoes, buttered toast and a mug of tea?' She could not resist the urge to get another dollop of sarcasm into the conversation.

Adam was ready for it, but chose to simply ignore it, so she continued: 'I'd love to. I've got some stuff to see to which will take a few days, but I'm free next Monday.'

'Excellent. I'll see you then. Shall we say seven o'clock?'

'Perfect. See ya. Bye!'

That was that. Lauren was back in Adam's life and all that remained before Monday, was to clean up the flat and decide what meal he would try to prepare. First thing in the morning, he would look up possible recipes online and perhaps have a couple of practice runs in order to make sure that he got it right on the night.

# SIXTEEN

Adam's timing was perfect and the meal of chicken risotto was ready within five minutes of her arrival at the flat.

They sat down to eat.

'Honestly, I wanted to text you so much after all that at Doug's, but I thought that you'd think I was a proper bitch.'

'It was my fault. I let those people get to me.' He wanted to use stronger language, but thought better of it. 'I lost my cool. It would've been better if I'd just shut up.'

Lauren smiled as she reached for some more wine. 'I don't blame you. Actually, Doug and I had a massive row about it afterwards. I was mad at him for what he said to you.'

'Is that why you broke up?'

'It wasn't the only thing, but it was sort of the beginning of the end, if you know what I mean. Can I be totally honest with you?' She set down her fork and looked straight at him.

'Come on, of course you can!'

'I'd been thinking about stuff for ages. Doug wanted me to be more like a wife than a girlfriend. I'm a student, for goodness sake. I was falling behind with my uni work and I want to have some laughs while I still can, before I get serious with anyone and have to find a job and all that. I should have ended it with him ages ago, but I didn't have the nerve. Anyway, I came home early from a lecture one day, and found him getting very familiar with my housemate, Amy.'

'Oh no!'

'Oh yes. It turns out that he's been dating some of my other mates as well. Some mates aren't they? Funny thing is that they all thought that he was only serious about them. The truth is that it's his boss, Vicky, who he really fancies. Apparently, she likes him – so she can keep him as far as I'm concerned.'

'Oh man, that's bad. I'm sorry. By the way, I thought you'd be going back to Sheffield for the summer holidays.'

'I should have gone weeks ago, but I needed to re-sit some exams and finish some course-work before I can go home. I passed, thank goodness, so my dad is going to come down and pick me up in a few days.'

'He's a good bloke, is your dad. Look, Lauren, before you go back home, can I tell you about some other stuff that's been going on?'

'Yes, please. Tell me.'

Adam told her everything about the meal at Wilders, the note, the arrival of the people in the van and his chat with Jed. After he'd finished, Lauren seemed not to know what to say and sat opposite him with horror on her face.

'Oh please, Adam, be careful. I'm really worried about you now. God knows what this Karol guy's capable of doing. Why don't you come back home to Sheffield with me and just pack all this in? You can stay at my place for a bit. My parents will be going to their caravan in Derbyshire. They go there most weekends. Dad likes his fishing and it's like having a home from home.'

'I'm tempted, but my life is down here now. Mum's gone, Jeff's got the flat and his new woman. You've got your studies to think about as well. I shouldn't have told you, but it's been bugging me.'

'I'm glad you feel that you can trust me. I promise I'm not part of any people-smuggling gang and I don't have a revolver in my bag! God, is that the time? It's going to take me ages to get home, so I'd better get going soon.'

Adam had planned for this point in the conversation and was ready. 'Why don't you stay here tonight? You can have my room and I'll sleep in Phil's bed. I reckon that he hasn't stayed here for more than one night in the last month and Jed's out, as usual.'

'Well if it's okay. I was a bit worried about going home on my own. Some of the streets near my place are a bit risky and...'

'What? Come on, tell me.'

'I was only going to say that Doug used to pick me up in his car, so I didn't ever really feel worried about getting home at night.'

'Well, you're okay tonight. In any case, I'd have gone with you, to make sure you got home safely.'

'Really? All the way across London?'

'Absolutely.'

'That's nice. Want a hand with the washing-up?'

As they dried the last of the dishes and cleared away the crockery, Adam felt a sense of relief that he had at last been able to share his secret. The big question was what, if anything, could be done about it?

# SEVENTEEN

Adam was up first and, within five minutes, had the bacon sizzling in the pan and the eggs ready to join it.

'Something smells nice.' Lauren emerged from his room soon after and over breakfast they discussed what their next move might be. Option one was to do nothing and for Lauren to go home and Adam to carry on as if nothing had happened. Option two was to try to help without getting into any danger themselves.

'I think you owe it to Helia to try to do something for her, even if it's only getting a photograph of these people and where they live and then letting the police or somebody know where they are. You can't do any more. You're great with bacon and eggs, but not with big men carrying guns!'

'You have a way of putting things, Lauren.' Adam was trying not to laugh at how she had managed to bring fried food into what was a serious issue.'

'I think I should try to find Helia and talk to her. If she can tell me where she lives, then I can just secretly pass on the address and hope that something gets done about it.'

'What did you do with the note?'

'I keep it hidden in my sock drawer.'

This time, it was Lauren who almost spat out her breakfast. 'Well it'll need to be specially cleaned after it's been in there. I can see people having to wear protective suits. They might have to evacuate the street first!'

Adam laughed. 'What I don't understand, is how these people organise all this without the police, or whoever, finding out.'

'Actually, we've been learning about that on my degree course. Know what an IP address is?'

'Not sure.'

'Know what the dark web is?'

'Ditto.' Adam disliked being made to feel uneducated and was becoming irritable.

'Know what an onion router does?'

'Onions? I fry them at Vera's.'

'Dear me!' Lauren was enjoying the look of puzzlement on Adam's face. 'Silly boy, it's software that allows criminals to share secret information without the good guys being able to trace them.'

'So you think they use this dark web thing to organise all their nasty stuff?'

'I'd say almost certainly, but that doesn't help us find Helia does it?'

A minute or two of silence passed as they thought, before Adam had an idea.

'How about if you go and have your nails polished or ears waxed, or whatever it is they do, at Katie's salon? I'll tell Tony that my friend would like to have her nails done and he might give me the address of the place. You go along and ask for Helia to do it. Try to pass a message to her and tell her that I need to know where she lives. Once I've got her address, I'll tell the police and they can help her and the others out.'

'So you want me to have my nails done and spy for you at the same time?' She put her knife and fork down. 'Would you ever want to go out with her again?'

'Well she is nice and I'd like to help her?'

Lauren seemed unconvinced at the plan and slightly jealous of Helia. Her eyes narrowed with doubt. 'And what will you be doing, while I am doing all this Jane Bond stuff?'

'I'll follow you and keep an eye on you from a distance. I mean, if you can't get to Helia then that's your part over and you'll have some lovely nails to show for it.'

'Paid for by you, I presume?'

Adam was enjoying this conversational tennis match. 'Paid for by me. On the house.'

'Well, I must say, my nails could do with some attention. Will you throw in an eyebrow shaping also, for free?'

'Go on then. I'll contact Tony and try to find out where I can find Helia. When I know the address of the salon I'll let you have it.'

# EIGHTEEN

The plan, however simple was ready to go, and after that all that Adam and Lauren intended to do was to locate Helia and try to find out where she and the others like her could be found. It was then only a matter of informing the authorities and letting them set these people free. Adam's dependence on Tony would have to be risked. His conscience would not allow him to carry on and just pretend that he knew nothing about the captives.

After having walked with Lauren to the station and receiving an extra long hug as payment for his hospitality, Adam messaged Tony.

Hi Tony. Hope you're ok. Thanks for the meal at Wilders by the way. I really like Helia and I want to take her out, alone LOL. TBH I REALLY like her, so could you sort out for her to meet me somewhere? Also, I know a girl who wants to have her nails done in a proper salon and all that. She's getting married and wants to look good before the wedding. Where does Helia work? Hope Katie's ok too. A.

Now it was a matter of waiting. If Tony didn't give Adam the address of the salon, then perhaps he might get it from her on their date, if it ever happened. The problem was that there were a lot of "ifs and buts" and Adam had no control over what happened next. Time was running short and he had to be back at work on Monday. To complicate matters further, Lauren's dad had arranged to come down in three days and take her back to Sheffield for the summer, so she would soon be gone.

At last, a message arrived at 3:29 a.m on Thursday morning.

Hi, bad news. Helia had to go back home to Finland. Her mum got sick and she's gone back to look after her. No idea when she'll be back in London. Depends on what's up. Sorry and all that. Don't know where your friend lives, but if she can get to Peppermints on Dronfield Street in Heston, she'll get 20 per cent off. Just has to tell them that she's a friend of Tony.

Adam read the message several times before being able to take in the news about Helia. He was sure that she had told him that she was from Norway. Tony's message said Finland so was this just a mistake on his part? Was it just bad luck that Helia had gone back now, so soon after passing the note to Adam? This situation meant a re-think and a call to Lauren was needed as a matter of urgency. There was then a knock on the door and, for a while at least, any plans to contact Helia or call Lauren were put on hold.

# NINETEEN

Adam opened the door, to find himself facing two smartly dressed women. The shorter one on the left was the first to speak,

'Good morning, sir. Are you Mr Adam Hicks?'

'Yes, I am.'

'I'm Detective Inspector Newsome from the Metropolitan Police and this is my colleague D.C. Howe. Could we come in? We'll only be a few minutes. We're trying to locate someone who we believe lives here. May we…?'

'Sure, please come in.'

Adam led them into the living room. Not for the first time that day, Adam found himself trying to make sense of what was going on around him.

Having refused the offer of a cup of tea, the visitors got straight to why they had called. Howe did the talking as Newsome stared intently at Adam.

'Can you tell us when you last saw your flatmate, Mr Jeremy Harding? You probably know him as Jed.'

Adam explained that both Jed and Phil, whilst officially living in the flat, tended to spend time away doing other things and that Jed earned extra money as a DJ. He hadn't seen Jed in five or six days, but that wasn't unusual. In the past Jed had booked time off without telling anybody and had gone home to see his children. As far as Adam knew, Jed was separated from the mother of his kids, but continued to support them financially.

Howe scribbled down some notes as Adam spoke, and this time it was the younger, but more senior, Newsome who spoke.

66

'Adam, I'm really sorry to have to tell you that we're really concerned for Jed's safety. Our colleagues in another area of London have found a body and we have reason to think that it might be Mr Harding. At the moment, we can't be sure it is him.'

'Oh no, that can't be right. It must be someone else!'

'We hope so, obviously,' she continued, 'but we'd like to take some of Mr Harding's personal possessions with us, in order to help us…' she paused and seemed to be searching for the best way of saying what she had to say. 'Well let's just say that in certain conditions, identifying a deceased person isn't always as easy as we wish it could be.'

'What do you want to take?' Adam felt like the walls of the room were closing in on him. His eyes began to fill with tears.

'Something that he might have used for personal care, perhaps a toothbrush or a hairbrush. We'd also like to take his laptop or iPad, if he had one. Do you know if he used that kind of device?'

'Everything of his is in his room over there. He was always on his laptop, looking at the photos of his kids. He had an iPad as well, I think.'

'Thanks. Before we do anything else, did you notice anything different about Jed over recent times? Did he seem stressed or worried?'

Adam told them that he hadn't noticed anything unusual. In fact, Jed rarely seemed to be anything else other than his usual cheerful and optimistic self. Jed's main focus had always been to earn enough money to support his children.

The two police officers listened with a sympathetic look on their faces before going in to Jed's room to put whatever they needed into evidence bags.

'What if Jed turns up? What do I tell him? He'll go mad when he finds out you've taken his laptop and all that.'

Howe answered. 'We'd love that to happen. It'd help us no end. If he does come home or make contact, please ask him to get in touch with us straight away and we'll send his stuff back. These kinds of things do happen from time to time, and, on some occasions, the missing person turns up safe and well. We'll leave a list of what we've taken and I'll give you this card with my number on it. Can I ask you not to discuss this with anyone. Jed's missing at this time and we really can't be sure if the person we've found is him.'

They left and Adam was alone again, with even more to think about. He desperately needed some fresh air and thought perhaps a walk might help him to piece together the events of the last few hours.

# TWENTY

Outside the flat, he turned right and walked up the road, in the opposite direction from his usual route to the Tube station. Wembley Stadium loomed high above the row of houses on his left and the flags around the rim of the stands snapped in the breeze. Though they were hidden by the houses, he could hear trains rattling along the railway cutting, some heading east towards Brent and others heading for Uxbridge in the west. On the other side of the road a party of children from a local Primary School were being shepherded through the gates of an urban farm by adults. Each child was wearing a high visibility jacket with the name of the school written in large writing on the back. The children walked in pairs, holding hands, and were noisily excited to be out of the classroom.

Vehicles passed by on the busy road and Adam looked at the faces of the drivers, each in their own safe metallic space. Some stared ahead, some talked on the phone and some were singing along to music. They were all oblivious to Adam gazing into their lives. Up ahead traffic came to a halt. One or two impatient motorists started to let off their horns to show their annoyance, but, however much they complained, nothing moved at all and Adam took pleasure at being able to amble past them. Suddenly he noticed that the stationary car next to him was the Maserati from the other night, outside Wilders. It was clearly the same car. Adam looked inside and the driver was the same man he saw at the restaurant. Two other men were in the back, and, for a moment, Adam's eyes and theirs were locked on each other. Mercifully, the traffic began to move again and the Maserati was soon out of sight. Adam felt the urge to change direction because the last thing he wanted to do was to catch up with that car again.

A few metres ahead there was a pedestrian crossing and he waited for the signal to change so he could get across to the other side of the road. At the end of a residential street he came across a footpath that ran adjacent to a narrow stretch of river and he decided to follow it along for a while to see where it took him. It seemed strange to find such a small oasis of peace among all of the traffic noise and fumes. A sign on the footpath told him that this was the River Brent and that the footpath was dedicated to the memory of a Councillor called Dave Green, who had campaigned for this area to be cleaned up and made into a place for local people to enjoy. 'Thanks Dave!' muttered Adam, as he watched water birds splashing happily in the river. A couple of hundred metres further, Adam found an empty park bench, and at last he was able to sit and start to organise his thoughts. This moment of peace did not last.

On the other side of the river, no more than thirty metres away, was another bench and sitting on it was the man he had seen in the Maserati. The stranger seemed to be totally oblivious of Adam and was talking on his phone. Who was he and why was he following him? Adam guessed that the man must be part of Tony's gang and that he had been assigned to keep a watch on Adam. Why was he was of so much interest to these people? He had not seen Helia again, and, to his knowledge, no one knew about the note. When he next looked across at the stranger, the bench was empty. Alarmed, Adam looked in every direction, but there was no sign of the stranger, or of anyone else. Again, the urge to get home and lock the door behind him, overpowered him and the walk home became more of a run. Once or twice, Adam sensed that someone was watching him, though there was no sign of the Maserati or anyone acting suspiciously.

Once he'd closed the flat door behind him he decided it was time to check on Lauren and make sure that she was safe and to tell her not to bother going to the salon. Her safety was all that really mattered to him.

# TWENTY-ONE

'We pay for their journey over here and give 'em work. These flipping foreigners, eh! What are we going to do with them? Offer them the chance to come over here and earn some cash. What's wrong with that?'

Tony was sitting in the armchair and facing the door as Adam came through into the lounge. In his hand, Tony was holding Helia's note and shaking his head. Adam thought of turning and running, but a man he recognised as the one from the park bench was now standing behind him and preventing any escape.

Tony continued. 'Y' know, I don't ask for much do I, Adam? I'm your kind old uncle Anthony... the bloke what's given you a new life. This place, a job, everything really. But what do I get in return?'

Adam tried to say something, but could find no words.

'I'll tell you shall I? All I want is for you to run my bloody little cafe. That's it. Keep your head down and work. Oh no, but you can't do that can you? So what do you do? You go and start taking secret notes from girls, under the table in *my* restaurant.'

Tony started to chuckle and was clearly enjoying Adam's discomfort. 'The funny thing is that we didn't expect her to try something like that. She was one what we had some hopes for. We thought she might have what it takes to work for us in moving more of 'em over here. She had good English, good contacts – the lot. Then she goes and blows it by asking you to help. Well, we were very upset weren't we Victor?'

The man standing behind Adam looked at the floor in mock sadness. 'Awful let-down, Tony. Such a shame.'

Tony recognised the man's joke and took it further.

'Ah well. We all make the odd mistake, Victor. Let's not be too hard on the lass. Oh – but you were a bit hard on her, weren't you? Where did you send her?'

Victor released a booming laugh that at any other time might have been that of some genial uncle at a family party, and suddenly he began to sing in a fine tenor voice, which belied his rugged features. His song had clearly been rehearsed and had entertained him for some time.

'*She left her heart near Newport Pagnell. High on a hill it calls to me.*'

By now Tony and Victor were close to hysterical with laughter and they both sang this line several times, before Tony brought the merriment to an abrupt end. He lunged across at Adam and gripped him tightly by the throat. 'Now let's get this clear my little nephew, the only reason you're not now with Helia is because you happen to be my sister's kid. If you weren't, then... well, let's just say life might be different.' Adam was gasping for air and Tony's grip remained tight around his throat. Tony hadn't finished.

'I'm going to give you one more chance. There's not many what gets one, believe you me. If you're willing to keep quiet, then I'll forget about all this. If you're nice to me, then there's a place for you in the team. I can see you being quite useful actually. We need a clean fresh- faced lad to manage some of our more legit businesses. God, you've so much to learn young fellow-me-lad. I'd be really upset if you went and told those two nice police ladies about this. Sadly for him, Jed thought he'd try to try and get some money from me with a threat to tell the law. Victor had a quiet word with him and Jed agreed to say nothing to anyone. Poor old Jed, I quite liked him. Now what do you say? Oh sorry, I'm stopping you breathing? Silly me.'

Tony released his grip on Adam's throat, but it was still some time before Adam could breathe clearly again.

'Okay, okay, please. Don't hurt me.' He gasped.

'Good, good. That's better. Oh, one more thing. Other than Jed, you didn't tell anyone about what you know. Did you?'

'Nobody else. Honestly.'

'Lovely. So you won't mind if Victor has a little look at your phone then? Victor, if you don't mind!'

Adam felt Victor's powerful grip on his arm and, before he could prevent it happening, his phone had been taken out of his pocket and was being handed to Tony.

In a second, Tony was scrolling through Adam's messages and recent calls.

'So who's Lauren? Hang on, wait a minute. She's not the one wanting her nails doing is she? You've sent her to the salon to...' Tony was piecing events together and forming a clear picture of what Adam and Lauren had planned.

'Please leave her out of this, Tony!'

'Well, all I can say is that me and Victor will have to have arrange to have a quiet little chat with this Lauren lass, just to make sure that she doesn't know anything. Anyway, I'll take this phone off you. Catch!'

Tony threw the phone over to Victor who put it inside his jacket.

'Right. Must be off. Let's not be a silly boy, Adam. To the car, Victor. We've got some texting to do, haven't we? Don't try to leave the flat, either '

The door closed behind them and Adam's only thought now was for Lauren. This time, there was no time to sit and think. She had to be warned of the danger she now faced.

# TWENTY-TWO

It was obvious that Adam would try to warn Lauren, and that the only way to alert her would be to go and tell her in person, so Tony had posted one of his men outside the flat to stop this from happening. Adam could only stare out of the window and wait. He waited all night and the morning traffic was at its height when the stranger finally left his post.

Weary and frantic, Adam raced into the street and desperately looked for a taxi. The only other person he could think of who might be willing to help was Doug, so he planned to head to Doug's place to try to convince him that Lauren was in serious danger.

All the black cabs that came past were occupied, and it was ten minutes before an empty one came along. Having given the driver the address, all Adam could do was sit back and wait as the taxi dodged and weaved through the London rush towards Clerkenwell. As if tormenting him, the lights seemed to turn red at every opportunity and buses pulled out in front of the cab, causing everyone behind them to slow down. The minutes dragged and it was over half an hour before the cab pulled up outside Doug's block.

Adam raced to the buzzer and pressed it furiously but no one answered. He tried several times, growing ever-more frantic, before trying one of the other flats in the hope that someone might know where Doug might be. Still no one answered. Was anyone actually at home in this place? At last, a sleepy voice came through the speaker: 'Who's that. Don't you know what time it is? If it's a delivery, leave it outside.'

'Please help. I'm sorry to disturb you but I need to

be able to find Doug from Flat 7. It's really urgent. Someone might die soon if I can't find him. I'm a friend of his and his girlfriend's in massive trouble. Please!'

There were a few moments of silence as the person upstairs took time to decide what to say next.

'You mean that girl who stays here? The pretty one? What's up with her?'

'You wouldn't believe me if I told you. I need Doug to help me find her. I just need to know where I can get hold of him.'

'I know where he works, if that's any use.'

'Yes, please.'

'His firm have an office in the JP Woodward Tower in Canary Wharf. The business is called Keele Investment Services. I know because I used to work there, but I've retired now. Does that help? Hello? Hello?'

Adam had already started to run down the road and was trying to hail another taxi. There was another agonising wait for a free cab to come by, but eventually Adam found himself en-route to Canary Wharf and the JP Woodward Tower. At least the taxi driver seemed to know where he was going. Yet again, everything that could hold them up seemed to decide that it would do just that.

As the taxi drew closer to Canary Wharf huge buildings loomed overhead, and the reflection of the sun in the millions of windows became disorienting.

'Here we are, son,' said the taxi driver, cheerily. 'That'll be fifteen quid. Cheers, pal. Have a good day.'

Adam looked above him at the countless floors climbing skywards. Doug was somewhere in there and he might well be the only hope of finding Lauren.

# TWENTY-THREE

As he approached the main entrance to the building, it became clear that, due to the level of security in place, getting in would not be easy. Adam could see that everyone who wished to enter needed to go through a security check and to show some proof of identity. He needed to find some way of looking like he had a legitimate reason to be allowed inside and, after twenty minutes, an opportunity came. Adam noticed that included among the many people approaching the building, there was a smartly dressed elderly man who was obviously somewhat unsteady on his feet and was also having difficulty managing the steps. Adam quickly stepped forward and said: 'May I help you?'

The man looked up and, to Adam's relief, answered: 'That would be very helpful. Thank you. Could you help me carry this bag? It's rather heavy.'

Adam guided the old man towards the entrance and, as they approached the check-point, the security official recognised him,

'Good morning, Mr Ashforth. How are you today?'

'I've had better mornings Eddie, but I'll survive,' said the old man with a smile. 'This young gentleman has kindly helped me up the last few steps.'

Before Adam had time to say anything, the security-man stepped aside and let both the old man and Adam through into the foyer, without asking for any identification. Adam was inside.

He noticed immediately how people seemed to be moving everywhere, like termites; everyone seemingly focused on their own business and oblivious to anyone else. Elevators and lifts took a constant stream of people to the upper floors and brought others back down. On the wall behind the reception desk, was a long list of all the businesses which were to be found in this tower and there were many of them. Adam stared at the list and tried to find Keele Investment Services. He eventually spotted their name and headed for the thirty-third floor.

He hurried to the lifts, feeling very out of place in jeans and trainers amongst all these hand-made suits and polished shoes. A ping signalled the arrival of the lift and Adam pushed his way to the front and got in. Several people in the lift gave him their most disparaging looks but he couldn't care less. The lift began its journey upwards, stopping at every floor, with people getting in and out. Twelve, thirteen, fourteen and still it kept stopping. Twenty-eight, twenty-nine, until at last it arrived at the thirty-third floor. Now where? Adam stepped out and found himself at the crossroads of four brightly lit corridors. Several businesses had their offices on here and Keele Investment Services was not one of them. At last, he arrived at a large glass door emblazoned with a large logo made from the letters KIS.

To his left was a reception desk, with a young man standing behind, speaking on a phone. The receptionist gestured to Adam, indicating that he would soon be able to help him, but Adam could not wait. Ignoring the receptionist's request to wait, he pushed through the door and into a large office area. At every desk, people were sitting at computer screens or were speaking through headsets, sometimes both. The buzz of conversations quietened as Adam shouted as loudly as he could.

'I want to see Doug. Is he here?'

A short man wearing thick-framed black glasses, stood from his seat and tried to force Adam back towards the door, but he pushed him back and moved through the office, calling out Doug's name.

There was now a clear sense of panic in the office and some people were leaving their seats and moving towards the exits. Once again Adam called Doug's name and this time, from behind a screen, Doug came towards him.

'What on earth are you doing here? Leave now before someone calls security. Come on, out!'

'Lauren's in big trouble, Doug. I've come to ask for your help.'

Doug turned to face his work colleagues, who were all watching to see what would happen, 'It's okay, everyone. Carry on. Panic over. I'll deal with this person, Please get on with whatever you're doing.'

The people slowly started to walk back to their workstations, though they were still eyeing Adam with some considerable wariness.

'You'd better not be messing me around. Come over here.' Doug gestured towards the screen and Adam followed him.

'Right, what's going on?'

Adam told Doug everything that had happened and Doug's face lost its colour. 'You idiot! Why did you have to involve her?'

'She wanted to help, that's why. I wouldn't have told her anything if I'd known that all this was going to happen. Look, I need your help. We need to find her.'

'I'll deal with you later. Let's get my car and drive to her place. She might still be there.'

Adam followed Doug out of the office to the lift. Doug pushed the button to send the lift to the lower ground floor and the below-ground car park.

'My car's there. Get in!'

Doug turned the ignition key, the engine roared and they were soon outside and battling through the traffic, heading north towards Lauren's flat. Adam had never visited Lauren's home and, every time he thought that they might soon be there, Doug kept driving on and on, further into the suburbs. Eventually and with a screech, they pulled up outside a row of terraced houses.

'Stay here, Adam. I'll go and ask if anyone knows where she is.'

'Thanks, but no. I'm coming too.'

The two of them approached the middle door on the terrace and knocked. After another impatient knock, someone inside appeared on the other side of the frosted glass.

'Who is it?'

'Is that you Amy? It's Doug. Open up, I need to ask you something.'

After chains were removed and a key turned in a lock, the door opened to reveal a young woman wearing a dressing gown and looking half-asleep.

'Doug? What's up? I thought you and Lauren had split up.'

'Never mind that. Have you any idea where she is?'

'Yes, she went out early this morning. She said that she'd had a text from someone called Alan? Adam? Anyway, she said he was in trouble and wanted to meet her.'

Doug turned to Adam and they both knew what had happened.

This time Adam spoke. 'Did she say where she was going?'

The girl could see the terror in their eyes.

'I think she might have said something about a beauty salon. Does that make sense?'

Doug turned to Adam. 'Well, does it to you?'

'I think so. Come on, we've got to get there quickly.'

'Where is this place?'

'Start the car and I'll tell you. I trust you've got a satnav in it?'

'Of course.'

Leaving the bemused young woman on her doorstep, Adam and Doug raced back to the car and Adam set about programming the satnav system for Dronfield Street in Heston.

Doug looked across at Adam. 'You know how far that is don't you? It's right over towards Heathrow Airport. It's bloody miles away. It'll take an hour to get there in all this traffic.'

Adam responded impatiently: 'Stop moaning and just drive,'

As they raced along, with Doug going through as many red lights as he could, a thought started to play on Adam's mind. It had to do with when Doug mentioned that Dronfield Street was out towards Heathrow, but he could not get the connection clear in his head.

Road signs for familiar places flashed by: King's Cross, Marylebone, Earls Court, Shepherd's Bush. Time dragged on and Heathrow Airport grew ever closer, until Doug took a sharp right and, after going under a railway bridge, he slowed down across the road from a tatty-looking nail bar.

'This is it. This is Dronfield Street. Look, that's Peppermints. Let's go in.'

Adam grasped Doug's wrist as he reached for the door handle. 'No, let's wait. If she was here, then she won't be now. They texted her hours ago and there's no way that they would have kept her here all day. Something tells me that if we wait here until they close, then we might be able to follow them and find out where they've taken her.'

As Adam spoke, his voice was drowned out by the deafening sound of a large aircraft that seemed only matter of a few metres above the car, approaching the runway. Such was the roar that everything rattled and whatever Doug saying was never reached Adam's ears. He finally realised what had been playing on his mind and, as if being electrocuted, he bellowed: 'Doug. That's it!'

Somehow, Doug had resisted the urge to throw him out of the car, though he now felt that that moment was rapidly approaching,

'What? Now listen, Adam. Let me tell you now that if one hair's been harmed on Lauren's head by your uncle and these lunatics, I'll skin you and give your bones to a dog.'

'Shut up, Doug, and listen,' Adam snapped. 'I think I know how to get to where they might be keeping her. The note that Helia gave me said that they can hear the noise of planes and that it's so noisy that things rattle. It's got to be near an airport. Somewhere on the flight path. Get it?'

'In case you don't know, London has a number of quite big airports,' said Doug dryly.

'Yes, I know. But, look, Helia worked here and other smuggled people will probably still be working here. This place is obviously on a flight path, so maybe they keep them somewhere close to work. They won't want to be driving them miles every day. It's all we've got so far.'

In the absence of anything else, Doug reluctantly agreed that Adam's theory might have some value,

'So we wait here then and follow whatever van or bus turns up and takes people away from here?'

'Yes, but I think we need to move down the road a bit. I think that we're a bit too noticeable sitting around here in a shiny silver Porsche.'

'Actually, to be precise, it's a Porsche 911 Carrera 4S Targa, and it's metallic agate grey, not silver. It's iconic and timeless and was designed to be a reflection of the past as well as a vision of...'

'Shut up and move it down the road a bit! All it does is draw attention to us and that's not good.'

Doug was offended by Adam's dismissal of his Porsche appreciation speech, but moved his car a little down the street and they settled to wait and see what happened at Peppermints.

Other than a handful of customers going inside and leaving an hour or two later, nothing much happened until around 3.30 when a young woman stepped through the door and looked up and down the road, before disappearing back inside. Ten minutes later it happened again, but this time it was another young woman who furtively looked up and down the road. It seemed they were waiting for someone to arrive. Adam recognised Katie as the third person to anxiously come outside and check that the coast was clear.

The time was close to four o'clock when a white mini-bus made its way around the corner and pulled up outside the salon. Phil got out of the driver's side and went in the building. Several minutes later, he re-emerged, opened the back door of the van and held it open as twelve people, both male and female, hurriedly scuttled out of Peppermints and climbed inside. Phil put his head inside to say something before slamming the door and getting back in the driver's seat.

'Right, Doug: when they move off, keep a reasonable distance behind them and try not to be obviously following them. I still think they won't go far.'

'This thing's got twin turbos and an extra light chassis, so they'll never get away from us. In fact, the bloke at the dealership told me that this particular model, has an electronic limited slip differential that detects wheel spin via a series of sensors.'

Adam rolled his eyes. 'Fascinating. Look they're moving away now, let them get around the corner before moving off.'

The mini-bus began to move away and turned left at the end of the road. Doug held back for several seconds before following it.

'Good. Nice and easy, Doug. Don't worry about anyone else getting between us and them, we can see where they're heading.'

The mini-bus weaved through back streets for twenty minutes and Doug kept the Porsche at a safe distance behind it, until, at last, it came to a halt at the end of a row of drab, terraced houses. The van pulled up outside one with a high wooden fence which hid the house from the footpath. All of the other houses had open front gardens, but, other than that, there was nothing to tell each house from the next. A Boeing 747 thundered just over the top of the houses, its under-carriage down and landing lights flashing.

'The sound of aircraft overhead, making everything rattle,' said Adam.

Reluctantly, Doug had to concede. 'I think you might be right about this place being where these people are being held. So what do we do now?'

By now Adam was aware of a side to himself that he had never seen before. He was determined to get inside the house and find Lauren, at whatever the risk to his own safety. He glanced over at Doug, and all he could see was a man consumed with the desire to drive expensive cars and acquire personal wealth and possessions. None of this mattered that much to Adam right then. All he wanted was to free Lauren and to help those people be able to live their lives without being used as human cargo by individuals such as Tony and the others. This was a challenge that would test him to the limit, but he felt ready to take it on.

'This is what we'll do, Doug – and don't even think about arguing with me. We'll drive past the mini-bus and park just around the corner. My guess is that Phil will drive into the backyard and that they use the back door to get them all inside. Look, that's what's happening. He's opening the gate, and then he'll drive as close to the door as he can, before he lets them out. Now drive past and park where we can't be seen.'

Doug drove past the house and parked around the corner in a place where no one in the house could see them, but from which they could still see the front door.

'I await your next instructions, sir!' said Doug, in an exaggerated robotic voice. Adam already had a plan.

'I've got to get in there and have a look. If she's not inside, then I've an idea where she might be, but, for now, let's take it one step at a time. When it's dark, you are going to drive this car into that wooden fence at the front of the house. Hopefully, one or more of the heavies will come out and leave the door open, I'll sneak in and see what's what.'

Doug's face dropped. 'What did you just say? You want me to drive my car. This beautiful Porsche 911 Carrera GTS with black leather interior and which is worth seventy-five thousand pounds, straight into that fence?'

'Yep! As fast as you dare, making sure that you make as much noise and do as much damage as you can. If they don't come out to have a look, then knock on the door and play the part of the bloke who just lost control and tell them how sorry you are. Daddy's just bought it for you and it's the first time you've taken it out on the road.'

'No chance!'

Adam now played his ace. 'How much do you miss Lauren? Do you still have feelings for her?'

'She ended it with me, don't forget. Want to know why?'

'She told me that she wasn't ready to be like your wife and that she wanted to enjoy her life as a free woman while she was still young.'

'That's not quite the full story. The truth is she really wanted to be with another man, and not me. She told me so.'

Adam was confused. 'Who? What other bloke?'

'Are you completely stupid? You. You're who she was talking about?'

For a moment, Adam was convinced Doug was joking, but the look on his face was too genuine for it to be a prank.

'Give up. Stop messing about.' Adam gazed into space.

'It's true. Anyway, in answer to your question, yes I

do have feelings for her, but I'm not sure I shouldn't just leave her to get on with her own life. For me, the biggest question is why would she be attracted to a bloke who works in a cafe serving bacon butties, when she could have all that I can offer her?'

'Dear me Doug! You really don't get it do you? Perhaps there is actually more to life than posh flats and shiny sports cars. Anyway, let's find her first and then we can have this chat again. As soon as it's dark I'm going to get out, hide, and then sneak inside.'

Five hours later it was dark enough for them to put their plan in play. At close to ten o'clock, Adam climbed out and positioned himself out of view, ready to dart inside the house as soon as the opportunity arose. Doug revved up the engine and, with the screech of Pirelli P Zero tyres on tarmac, the Porsche was hurled into the wooden fence.

# TWENTY-FOUR

There was a sickening sound of metal twisting, wood splintering and glass shattering. Adam could barely look as Doug's car was embedded in the wooden fence. Doug climbed out and surveyed the self-inflicted damage with tears in his eyes.

It did not take long before the front door of the house opened and Phil came charging towards the crumpled sports car in the ruined fence. Adam could not hear the conversation between Doug and Phil but there was a great deal of finger pointing and arm-waving taking place. Phil was gesturing up and down the road at the road, as if trying to understand how this accident came about. Doug looked as if he was blaming oil on the road to explain how the car had skidded and come to a halt where it now was. As Adam hoped would happen, two other men came out of the house and joined in the heated debate. This was his chance. With Doug and the others facing the other way, he climbed over the fence, sprinted across the open space to the house, and without hesitating went inside.

He immediately felt sick, not just because of the stench, but because of what he could see. The first room he walked into, had been divided into two large cages and the people had been clearly been separated into male and female sides. In one half, several women and young girls were sitting around as some small children lay asleep in what looked like dog beds. Used nappies littered the inside of their space, near the door, as if awaiting collection. In the other half of the room, a number of men were listlessly sitting cross-legged on the floor of their own cage. Some of them were looking over at the "female" side.

Adam knew he could not leave these people here. He had to do something for them and quickly. Several of the men quickly sat up and ran to the door of their cage, shouting and gesturing wildly to be allowed out. The cage was padlocked. Looking around, in the gloom he could see something hanging on a hook next to the door: a bunch of keys. Having snatched them off the hook, he hurried to the cage and set about trying to find the key to fit that lock. With trembling hands and clumsy fingers he tried four keys before eventually one fitted and the padlocked snapped open.

'Get out. Get out!' he shouted, as the captives jostled to be the first out of the door. One of the men gripped Adam's arm. 'My wife and child are in there. Help me get them out. Please.'

By now, those in the female side had realised what was going on and they too had rushed to the cage door and were screaming to be allowed out. For what seemed like forever, Adam desperately tried to find the key, but by now the noise coming from the house had alerted Phil and the others that something was wrong and their suspicions were confirmed by a rush of bedraggled people heading through the front door and out into the street.

'Jacko, get inside and stop any others from getting out,' shouted Phil. 'Keep the women in there. We'll be there in a minute'

Jacko saw Adam struggling to open the cage and pulled a knife from his pocket, flicked open the blade and stepped towards Adam.

'Give me those keys, kid. Now!'

Adam watched the blade coming ever closer to

him. Jacko's eyes remained fastened on his. Only seconds remained until the keys would be taken from him, so Adam pushed them through the bars of the cage out of reach. One of the women inside picked them up and slipped them into her pocket.

'That's a really bad idea.' Jacko lunged at Adam with the knife and as the cold blade grew closer, Adam closed his eyes and waited for the pain to begin. Instead, he heard the sound of the knife falling to the floor and, as he opened his eyes, he saw Jacko's facial expression freeze as his knees gave way beneath him. Sunk deep into the middle of his back, was a blade.

'Are you okay, my friend?' It was the man from the other cage.

'Yes. I think so,' Adam answered, shakily.

'You helped me out and so I help you in return. I don't care what happens to me now. Let's get them out. See? That's my wife there. We're coming. Pass us the keys.'

Within a minute, the cage was open and the women and dazed children made their way through the door and out into the night.

# TWENTY-FIVE

Adam and Doug found themselves standing alone in the dark. Both of them had tried to form a coherent sentence, but had given up and had retreated into their own thoughts. They were jolted back to reality by the arrival of the police, ambulances and two fire engines.

After ordering some uniformed police officers to enter the building, Newsome came over to Adam.

'What are you doing here?' she asked.

Doug was able to find an answer: 'We've been looking for someone, who this lot have probably got locked up somewhere.'

Newsome opened the rear door of her car and said, 'Get in and let's try to piece together what's been going on.'

The whole story spilled out of Adam and on two occasions Newsome needed to ask him to slow down so that she could try to make sense of it. When he'd finished, she turned to face Adam and Doug,

'This is going to take a lot of clearing up, in more ways than one. And don't you two start thinking that you're heroes either; in fact I think you're bloody idiots for failing to inform us of all this from the start.'

'We came to look for Lauren,' croaked Adam, 'She's not in there.'

Newsome had her head in her hands. 'I was supposed to be bloody going off duty an hour ago – forget I said that. I'm sorry. Right, let's focus shall we? You think these guys have taken your friend Lauren somewhere, do you?'

'I know they have. Tony took my phone and pretended to be me. I think he arranged to meet her somewhere. He's taken her, I know it.'

Doug added, looking at Adam: 'And if he has hurt her you can charge me with murder, because I'll have killed this scruffy little toad.'

Trying not to smile, Newsome looked at them in the mirror,

'Do either of you have any thoughts as to where they may have taken her?'

'Oh god! She's probably at Vera's. That's where this first started and there's some rooms upstairs, where it looks like they keep these people.'

'Where's Vera's? And what is it?'

Adam gave the address and Newsome reached for her radio.

'This is Tango Charlie Alpha. All available units to go to Vera's cafe on Sterne Street. Armed back-up will be required. Repeat armed back-up will be required. We have a possible hostage situation, so no sirens. We'll also need ambulances on stand-by, and make sure to put a cordon around the area. I want surrounding roads sealed off. Wait for me to arrive. I am on my way there.'

# TWENTY-SIX

Neither Adam nor Doug looked at each other, as Newsome drove at high speed towards Shepherd's Bush. Adam attempted to start a conversation, but did not get far,

'Listen, Doug, when this is all over let's... '

'Be quiet,' snapped Doug.

Adam gave up trying to build bridges. After all, not only had he smashed up his flat, but he'd now persuaded Doug to deliberately wreck his treasured sports car by driving into a fence at high speed and put his former girlfriend in mortal danger. There seemed no hope that this could ever be a lasting friendship.

By the time they reached Sterne Street, the area around Vera's had been cordoned off and dozens of police personnel surrounded the cafe. Doug and Adam were ordered to stay well back and behind one of the vehicles blocking off the road.

On the radio, Newsome was informed that repeated attempts to call the number had not been answered, but there was a light on in one of the upstairs rooms and that someone was in there.

'I definitely saw a gun in one of the desk drawers,' repeated Adam.

Newsome raised her eyebrows. 'At least we know that now. I think we need to act quickly. Stay here and do not move!' She slipped stealthily to behind a car that had been parked across the road from the front door. Adam could see that she seemed to be organising an attack on the building. They were going to move in.

Four armed figures moved quietly to a place next to the front door of the café, and a hydraulic jack was set up to breach the door. There followed much shouting and commotion, and the sound of breaking glass and furniture being thrown around. Then two shots rang out, followed by total silence. From where she crouched, Newsome ran across the road and inside the cafe. The dam of Adam's resistance broke and he could not resist the urge to rush in after her.

Everyone at the scene outside of Vera's seemed so focused on what they were doing, that no one challenged him and he was able to run inside without being stopped. By now everyone involved in the raid seemed to have gone upstairs and so he followed. Adam had only got half way up the stairs when a voice from above said: 'Get back down these stairs. This is a crime scene. Get out now!'

'I want to see if my friend is in here,' he pleaded.

'Whoever you are, wait outside, this area is not safe. Get out and stay behind the cordon. Go!'

As Adam reluctantly turned to go back down, some paramedics bustled upstairs and past him on the narrow stairway. As he reached the bottom of the stairs, he was sure that he heard someone say there were two casualties, one female and the other male.

'Work on the female first, it's too late for him now but you might just save her.'

It had to be Lauren and, his worse fears were confirmed, after an agonising wait, when she was brought out on a stretcher and put into an ambulance. Her face was distorted and almost swollen beyond recognition behind the oxygen mask. Adam stared at her and felt sick with guilt. The ambulance doors closed and she was taken away.

Doug appeared, also looking pale with worry. He too had seen Lauren and had also worked out that she was in a very bad way. Doug put his arm around

Adam's shoulders.

'Come on. Let's find out where they've taken her and wait for any news. She's going to need both of us for a while. I'll see if I can get us a lift to the hospital.'

# TWENTY-SEVEN

Lauren was taken straight into the operating theatre and it was a long time before anyone was able to give Adam and Doug an indication as to how well it was going. It was close to six in the morning when D.C. Howe came down the hospital corridor, deep in conversation with a doctor. Adam got up and approached them,

'How's Lauren? Can you tell us anything?'

D.C. Howe and the doctor exchanged glances. The type when two people seem to be sharing a secret and have been sworn not to share it, but Howe felt obliged to say something,

'Okay, well, she's out of theatre and she's been what they call stabilised, meaning that Doctor Curran here and her team have been able to give her a real chance of pulling through. The bad news is that she's suffered some really awful injuries and it's going to be touch and go for a few days. Why don't you two just go home and we'll keep you informed. Both of you have got a big part to play in what happens next and we're going to want to speak to you in the near future.'

'No!' came the simultaneous reply from both.

'Well that's up to you, but nothing much is going to change for several hours yet. Oh, by the way, we've contacted Lauren's parents and they're on the way. I'll leave you for now. If you two want to stay around, that's up to you.'

With that, D.C. Howe continued down the corridor, through some double doors and out of sight.

So Adam and Doug settled down for a long wait and Lauren continued her fight to stay alive.

# TWENTY-EIGHT

Doug was snoring, with his head resting on Adam's shoulders, when Adam felt a gentle tap on his hand. 'Hello? Sorry to have to wake you, but I thought you'd want to know how she is.'

It took several seconds for his eyes to fully open and for a clear picture to form, but at last Adam could recognise the outline of Doctor Curran through the mist of semi-consciousness.

'Is she okay?'

'Lauren is conscious, which is obviously good, but she's still very poorly. Her mum and dad have arrived and are down there and in the room with her. It's ten o'clock and I know that you two have been here all night. D.I. Newsome is around, but I've told her that it's too early to be asking Lauren any questions. If you want, I could ask her to come and have a word.'

'That'd be helpful. Thanks,' Adam said sleepily.

Newsome arrived in less than five minutes and she was clearly tired and anxious.

'Still here? I admire your persistence but I think you two should go home and get some rest. I'm heading in your direction, Adam – so I'll drop you off at your place.'

'What about sleeping beauty here?' Adam gestured at the still sleeping and snoring Doug.

'I'll arrange for him to be taken home as well. He's going to be busy trying to get his car back and it's mainly you who we need to talk to.'

Doug was woken up and helped to a car, while Adam and Newsome made their way to Wembley and to Adam's flat.

Newsome was not one for small talk. She confirmed that Tony was still on the run. It looked very much like he had forcibly taken Lauren to Vera's and had left her with Karol. She did not want to give any details on what Lauren had gone through and they had just got there in time to prevent Karol from killing Lauren.

'Mr Nowak, or Karol as you knew him, is now sadly deceased and so obviously won't be able to help us.'

'What about Jed? What about Helia?'

With her now familiar matter of fact manner, Newsome answered, 'I'm sorry to be the one who has to tell you that Jed's was indeed the body that we found recently. His remains have been formally identified by his ex-partner and we can assume that he was killed by a member of this particular group of individuals. As for the girl you know as Helia, we really don't know who she was. These people are seldom known by their actual names. We think it's unlikely that she will have escaped. I fear the worst.'

'Oh, that's my fault again. I told Jed everything that I'd seen in the cafe. Tony said something about dealing with Jed.' They arrived at the flat and got out of the car. 'I don't want to seem tactless, but I've also been thinking that I'll have to leave this flat before long.'

'Afraid so. I'd say that no one will do much for a few weeks, so you've got a little while to find somewhere else to live.'

'Marvellous.'

'One last thing,' said Newsome as she was turning to leave, 'you're incredibly lucky to still be here now. These people will kill someone without thinking twice. We're having to deal with dozens of criminal organisations like this. London is full of people who've been trafficked illegally into this country and who are being used to run businesses like Vera's or Peppermints. These migrants are no more than slaves. What you saw in the house, isn't unusual at all, and if any of the captives try to escape or get help, well you can guess the rest. Have you ever given any money to someone begging in the street?'

'Now and again, yes.'

'I'm not trying to stop you, just remember that many of these poor people are forced to beg for money, by monsters like your uncle and his friends. You might want to bear that in mind.'

'Do you know where Tony might be?'

'No. Not at this time. We suspect that he's gone to ground somewhere and that he'll try to get abroad. His criminal organisation is now dead, so he'll be licking his wounds for a while. We'll have him soon enough. You can sleep easy.'

# TWENTY-NINE

A week passed and Adam called the hospital every day for news on Lauren's condition. He was told that she was making a slow recovery and that, at present, only close family members were allowed to visit her. Two further weeks passed and his luck eventually changed, when he was told that she was well enough to see other visitors, and, within two hours, he was outside her room and waiting for her parents to finish their visit. There was only five minutes of visiting time left, when the door opened and they walked down the corridor towards him.

Lauren's mother smiled as she saw him standing and waiting. Adam could see a close resemblance between mother and daughter.

'Hello. You must be Adam. I'm Anne and this is Lauren's dad, Mark. Thanks for coming to see her.'

'How is she?' Adam asked.

Lauren's dad answered. 'It's going to be a long time before she'll be anywhere close to the way she was, but she's getting the very best care and we'll see that she gets whatever she needs.'

For a brief moment, Adam wondered if Lauren's parents might not want him to go in, but Lauren's mother put his mind at ease by adding: 'She's been asking if we know where you are. She'll be really happy to see you. We're off to our hotel for a rest, until the next visiting time. She'll be really happy to see you. Bye.' Lauren's parents left and Adam went in.

Lauren was sitting up in bed, with her eyes closed. Her face was little more than a network of jagged wounds, extending across her cheeks and around her mouth. A bandage covered her head and extended down over her left ear, with some extra protection over it. To her left, bank of monitors bleeped her vital signs.

Adam hesitated and thought about leaving, but when she realised that someone had come into the room, Lauren opened her eyes and saw him. Immediately, her eyes opened wide and her hand reached to the edge of her bed. Without hesitation, Adam stepped forward and held it.

'Lauren. I'm so sorry. I shouldn't have involved you in this. Please forgive me.'

Lauren attempted to turn towards him and as she did, she gently squeezed his hand. It looked, to Adam, as if she was trying to smile.

Adam told her about what had happened to Doug's car and how he had found and helped release the prisoners. Lauren's grip on his hand tightened when he came to describe the frantic journey to Vera's and how he felt when he heard the gunfire.

'I'll always be there for you Lauren, whenever you need me, just ask. One day you'll be better, and when you are, we'll go back into those woods and I'll prove to you that I can manage to jump over a raging stream.'

She gripped his hand even tighter and he noticed that her eyes seemed to be looking in the direction of the bedside cabinet. It seemed clear to Adam, that she wanted something from it. A drink perhaps, or a tissue from the box of tissues on top? Whatever Adam suggested seemed not to be right and he realised she was trying to show or tell him something.

'It is in the drawer?'

Her hand again tightened on his.

'Shall I look inside?'

She gripped again and painfully, tried to nod her head.

Adam opened the drawer and all he could see in it was a bible and a pen, which he took out. In the bottom of the drawer was a key.

'Is this what you want?'

Lauren's expression changed and her eyes locked on to his.

'What is this key for? Do you want me to take it?'

She pushed the key tightly into the palm, with what seemed like the last bit of strength she had. Still puzzled, Adam said, 'I'll look after this for you Lauren. I've no idea what it's for, but I'll keep it safe until you want it back.'

The moment was ended by the arrival of a nurse in the room, with a trolley bearing fresh bandages and other medical equipment.

'Looks like I've got to go now,' said Adam, 'but I'll come and see you again.'

Lauren's eyes widened again and he hoped that she was trying to show that she wanted him to stay, but it was clear that visiting time was over and that he must go. Lauren was still looking at him as he turned to her and waved.

# THIRTY

By early September the doctors had decided that Lauren was well enough to leave hospital and to return to Sheffield, where her parents had agreed to care for her. Dr Curran had made it clear that Lauren's recovery was going to be slow and that there would be setbacks along the way, but agreed that home was the best place for her to be.

Adam had failed to find another job in London and, as he expected, he was required to leave the flat. There was no other option open for him than to return to Sheffield and to move into his old bedroom. He tried to make contact with Jeff and Carol, but whenever he rang, there was no answer, and so, with some sadness, he boarded a coach and made his way north. His plan was to go to and visit Lauren as soon as possible.

'I'm so sorry, Adam, but it's not possible right now.' Carol stepped out onto the landing and carefully closed the door of the flat behind her, so that no one inside could hear what she had to say,

'It's Jeff. He's really poorly and it's really not going to be possible for anyone to stay here at the moment. I've just sent for an ambulance because he's really struggling today. I'm really worried. Do you want to go in and have a word with him? I think you should.'

Adam barely had time to decide what to think, before Carol took his arm and led him into the lounge, where Jeff was laying on the sofa. Had Adam not known Jeff so well, he would have had difficulty recognising the man who had come into his life all those years ago. Jeff was now little more than a skeleton with a tight grey covering of skin and the sunken eyes of someone close to death. Unsurprisingly, between gulps of air, Jeff's greeting was predictable and he went on the attack, rasping: 'What are you doing here? I thought I'd told you to stay away.'

Before Adam could react to this latest bout of hostility, Carol leant over to wipe some perspiration from Jeff's forehead,

'Stop it Jeff! We've been over this and you agreed to try and to be civil to Adam, so please make an effort to be pleasant.'

'I hear your uncle turned out to be a bad 'un,' Jeff whispered. 'I knew all along he was crooked. I told your mother that he was, but she wouldn't listen... Is that why you're back here? You want somewhere to stay again, do you?'

'No, it's okay, Jeff. I won't bother you.' Adam could not find it in his heart to get into an argument with someone who was obviously so sick. He turned to leave and Carol followed him outside.

'I'm sorry, Carol. I wouldn't have come if I'd known things were like this. The truth is that I don't have anywhere else to stay. It all went wrong down in London, but I'll sort something out. Look after yourself.'

With that, Adam turned and went back down the staircase, certain in his mind that he would not return. Now he needed somewhere to live.

# THIRTY-ONE

'Thank God for Sam!' Adam said to himself, as he finished off a plate that, a few minutes before, had been piled high with chicken pie and vegetables. Sam had agreed to let Adam stay at his house until he was able to find somewhere more permanent.

Sam had decided not to go to university, but instead to follow his passion for food, and was now working as a chef at a hotel in the centre of Sheffield. He was pleased to be able to help Adam, having recently broken up with his girlfriend and was in need of some company. The arrangement was for Adam to stay with him, for as long as he needed, providing that he kept the place clean and chipped-in with money for food, when it became possible.

'So what are your plans then?' asked Sam.

'Firstly, I need to go and see Lauren and see how she is. I'll call her first and make sure that it's okay to go.'

'You really care for her, don't you?'

'You have no idea how much. Not a clue!'

The next morning, Adam called Lauren's home and her mother answered,

'Hi, Adam. I'm sorry but things have changed a bit since you last saw her. She's really not in a good place right now.'

'Why? What's wrong?'

'Physically, she's much better, but all this has affected her in other ways.'

'What do you mean?'

'I don't want to go through it all now on the phone, but I'm sure it'd cheer her up if you could come around.'

An hour later Adam was standing on the doorstep of Lauren's home. Her mum opened the door and smiled.

'You don't mess about, do you? Come in and I'll make you a coffee. She's upstairs at the moment, but I'll tell her that you're here.'

Adam sat at the kitchen table, sipping his coffee, as Lauren's mum went upstairs to tell Lauren that he was waiting downstairs. Adam could hear voice upstairs, but was unable to tell what they were saying. Several minutes later, Lauren's mum returned,

'She won't be a moment, Adam. So, how are you doing?'

Adam told her about having to move back to Sheffield and about Sam letting him stay there, until he'd sorted himself out. Lauren's mum listened with sympathetic eyes.

'On the job front, Adam: Mark may have some good news. He's at work now, but I'll ask him to speak to you when he gets home. Look, here she is...'

Lauren was standing at the kitchen door, her eyes fixed on Adam, twirling her hair between her fingers.

Lauren's mum got up to leave the room saying, 'I'll leave you two in peace. There's a lot to catch up with, I'm sure.' She bustled out of the kitchen, leaving Adam and Lauren alone.

Adam spoke first. 'Hi. How are you?'

'Fine. Great thanks. You okay?'

'Yeah!'

'Back in Sheffield, then?'

'Yep.'

'Nice day isn't it?'

'Come here, please.'

They stepped towards each other and embraced.

Neither spoke for some time and the only sound was the ticking of the kitchen clock on the wall. Adam could feel the tension in Lauren's body as she clung to him and as she turned her face to look at him, she was crying.

'What's up?'

'I'm fine. Honestly, I'm just a bit tired that's all'

'Sure?'

'Sure... Of course. So I gather that you're living with Sam these days.'

'For a while, yes. Until something better comes along and I can get some cash together and find somewhere of my own.'

'I'm sorry, Adam.'

'What for?'

'It's my fault that you lost everything you had in London. I should have been more careful and not got in Tony's car and... '

'Stop that right now,' Adam looked her straight in the eyes, 'It wasn't your fault. Any of it. I'm the one who got you involved. I'm the one who came up with the idea of trying to contact Helia. Bloody hell, Lauren, I almost got you killed!'

'What a pair we are, eh?'

'What do you mean?'

'We were pretty crap at being detectives, weren't we?'

This was the first that Adam had seen of Lauren's smile, but beneath it he sensed that she was still haunted by what she'd been through. He had an idea.

'Fancy going for a walk? The park looked nice as I came here. I'll buy you an ice cream.'

'No. It's okay. I'll stay here. You go if you want. I'm not in the mood.'

'Come on Lauren, it'll be… '

'No. I don't want to. Please Adam. I can't… I mean… '

Adam waited for her to finish her sentence, but it remained incomplete and lost. She seemed to be a prisoner inside her thoughts and another long period of silence was only broken by the rustling of letters being pushed through the letter box and dropping onto the doormat.

'I'll go home now,' Adam said. 'I've upset you and you know that's the last thing I want to do.'

'No. Please stay. I'm sorry. It's just the thought of seeing lots of people… I'm happy to be with you, I really am. Don't go.'

Adam and Lauren spent the next few hours watching TV with the curtains closed. Lauren seemed happy to sit and hold Adam's hand as the hours of daytime programmes came and went. When the news came on, she changed channels and seemed more comfortable with watching people talking about antiques or recipes. Adam noticed that she gripped his hand slightly tighter when a trailer came on for an American police drama, in which people drew guns and fired them at each other.

The rest of the afternoon passed, and, despite several attempts to leave, Lauren would not let Adam go. In the end, Adam insisted that he had to go home, and Lauren reluctantly agreed, but with the promise that he would be back the next day.

As he was stepping through the door to go home, Lauren's mum asked: 'Well Adam, how does she seem to you?'

'Quiet and nervous, is how I'd put it.'

'That's exactly right. She's really snappy at times

and she won't leave the house, not even to go into the garden. Did you notice how pale she looks? We've been to see her doctor and she's suggested counselling of some kind, but she won't agree to it. To be honest Adam, she's been much better with you around. Mark's off work tomorrow, so please come again and I'll remind him to speak to you about the work situation.'

'I'll be back tomorrow,' said Adam. 'And I'll do what I can. I want to see Lauren back to being herself as well.'

# THIRTY-TWO

Adam arrived at nine the next morning and Lauren's dad let him in.

'Want a coffee?'

'Yes, please. Where is she?'

'She's in the front room… Adam, before you go through, there's something I want to ask you. Sit down a minute and let's chat for a minute.'

'Okay.'

Lauren's dad sat opposite Adam at the kitchen table and got straight to the point.

'Adam, I was talking to the manager at the golf club, over the weekend and I happened to mention that you were looking for work. Well, it turns out that he's looking for someone to cover for Claire, who's going on maternity leave. She runs the cafe and does the catering for club social evenings. I mentioned you and he's really keen to have a chat. What do you think?'

'I'd love to do it.'

'Brilliant! I'll text him in a bit and let him know. Oh and there's something else.'

'Yes?'

'We were wondering whether you want to move in here. Just lately, things have been a bit rough for Lauren and she's not doing so well. It'd be great if you were around her more. She's a lot more settled when you are.'

'She seemed okay yesterday… '

'Perhaps she said she was, but the truth is far from that. She's up most nights, pacing around her bedroom. She needs professional help, but she just won't take it. Will you have a go at persuading her?'

'Of course I will. Are you sure you're okay with me moving in?'

'Put it this way, I'll get the car now and we'll go and get your stuff from Sam's.'

---

Over the next week, Adam settled in to living at Lauren's house. The spare bedroom was spacious and there was ample room in the wardrobe for his clothes. The manager at the golf club, was suitably impressed with Adam's experience and wanted him to start immediately. The contract was initially for six months, with a review at the end, depending on whether Claire wanted to return or not. He would work from ten in the morning until five in the evening three days per week and all day Saturday.

Adam was quickly into the routine of working and spending the rest of his time with Lauren, and him being around seemed to help her relax, enough to consider the possibility of getting help. Adam saw his opportunity, just after tea one evening.

'Lauren?'

'Yes?'

'Please don't shout at me.'

'What have you done? I'm worried now.'

'Nothing. I haven't done anything, it's just that I want you to go and see the counsellor at your doctor's surgery. I'll come with you and wait outside. Please do it for me. If you don't like it, then you can stop. What do you think?'

Rather than storming off and becoming distressed, like she had been doing over recent weeks, Lauren calmly got up and left the room, leaving Adam to sit alone, wondering what her response would be. He decided not to follow her, but to be patient.

Fifteen minutes later, Lauren came back and sat next to him.

'I've been thinking,' she said. 'I'll give it a go. I can't go on like this. It's just that...'

'What?'

'I'm not Lauren any more. I feel like I'm just this empty shell where Lauren used to be. This time last year, I had everything ahead of me. Life in London, a super-rich boyfriend with a sports car...'

'Excuse me?' Adam recognised this as a flash of the old Lauren. 'Look, I can't say that seeing someone will definitely help, but you have to try to take every bit of support that's on offer.'

'Pass me my phone and I'll call the surgery and see if there are any appointments going spare. You will come with me? Promise?'

'Promise!'

A week later and Adam and Lauren found themselves sitting outside a door, above the doctor's surgery. On a low table next to their chairs, a radio was tuned into a "soft-rock" radio station and was playing hits from the 1980s, which they both hated. Adam wanted to switch it off or re-tune it, but a notice pinned to the wall above it read:

*"Please do not touch this radio!"*

'Shame, because I hate the bloody Bee Gees!' thought Adam.

At precisely five forty-five, the door opened and a woman with long grey hair, put her head around and said, 'Lauren? Hi, I'm Sharon, please come in.'

Lauren went inside and Adam sat through thirty more minutes of Elton John, Queen and other relics of a bygone age.

Eventually the door opened and Lauren stepped out.

As they were leaving, Adam asked: 'Well?'

'Well what?'

'How was it?'

'Let's go out and I'll tell you.'

'I'll book an Uber, and let's get home.'

Later that evening, after their meal, Lauren described her meeting with the counsellor.

'Well, it was better than I thought it might be. I sat on a sofa and she sat opposite me, making notes. I did most of the talking and she just listened. She wanted to know all about my life: friends, family, interests, and all that stuff. We didn't discuss anything else really. Nothing about... well you know... London.'

'Are you going to see her again?' asked her mum.

'Yes. Same time in two weeks.'

Adam smiled. 'Lauren, I'm proud of you.'

'Me too,' added her dad.

# THIRTY-THREE

As a rule, once he was in bed, few things ever disturbed Adam, but on this particular night something would not let him relax. Eventually, after several unsuccessful attempts to get to sleep, he switched on his bedside lamp and sat up in bed. Once his brain had fully cleared, from somewhere outside of his room he was sure that he could hear what sounded like someone sobbing. He got up and opened the door.

Lauren was sitting on the floor outside of his room, with her head in her hands. Adam knelt beside her and put his arm around her. In the dark he could feel her shaking, so he helped her up and into bed.

'Stay with me, Adam. I saw him and he wants to do it again.'

'Who do you mean?'

'It was Karol. He was standing right where you are. I could see his eyes staring at me. I could smell his breath... Adam, make him go away!'

'No, Lauren. He's dead and he can't hurt you now. It's over. Hold my hand and close your eyes. That's better.'

Adam sat beside her for an hour, holding her hand, until he was sure that she was settled, before going back to his room and eventually getting some sleep of his own.

Over breakfast, while they were alone, Adam told Lauren's dad about what had happened during the night.

'That's not unusual, Adam. She has these flashbacks and nightmares, quite regularly, in which she re-lives what happened to her. Her mum and I have been up many times and sat with her, sometimes right through night. Anyway, I really appreciate what you did. Honestly, neither of us heard a thing, or we would have got up and helped.'

'It's fine,' said Adam, 'at least she's still keeping these appointments with the counsellor. She's going tonight actually, so I'll go with her and wait.'

Later that evening, Lauren came out of the counselling session, holding several leaflets and some notes that the counsellor had made for her to read.

'What have you got there?' asked Adam,

'Sharon wrote down the name of various websites, that help people cope with anxiety and trauma, so I thought I'd try them out. There's even an App that you can download onto your phone, which gives you exercises that aid relaxation and help you find peace.'

'That's great. You seem positive about it.'

'You're right, I am. She says that it might take months or longer before I'll start to feel totally myself again, but that the more I do for myself then the better it is for me. Tomorrow I begin to practise mindfulness!'

'Mindfulness? What's that?'

'I have no idea. One of these leaflets explains what it is, and I'm going to try it.'

# THIRTY-FOUR

By Christmas, Lauren was approaching the end of her counselling programme and had started to feel confident enough to go on her own, to the local shops. She described how she sometimes imagined that everyone was looking at her, but was managing to identify when she was starting to feel anxious and to use the various techniques she'd learned to help her get through it.

Christmas day arrived, and after dinner, when Adam and Lauren's mum had cleared the table and filled the dishwasher, it was time to play some board games and to watch a DVD or two. It was Lauren's dad's choice this year and he opted for a spaghetti western, in which Clint Eastwood rides into town and kills the bandits who have been terrorising innocent people.

'I enjoyed that,' said Lauren's dad, before realising that everyone had fallen asleep.

Over the holiday period, Adam was kept busy at the golf club and did not get much time off, but was able to finish at eleven o'clock on New Year's Eve. Lauren had asked him to buy some fireworks to celebrate the arrival of the New Year.

'Shall we let them off in the garden?' he asked Lauren, when he got home.

'I fancy going into the woods, just you and me, and having our own fireworks display in there. What do you think? I've got a bottle of wine.'

'Sounds great, get your coat. It's twenty to twelve.'

They walked the short distance to the park and as Big Ben reached midnight on his phone, Adam set off the firework with the loudest explosion, which was matched by those from everywhere around. Rockets roared into the dark sky and drunken voices shared Auld Lang Syne.

'Happy New Year.'

'Thank you, Adam. You're the best thing that has ever happened to me.'

After finishing the bottle, they weaved a rather unsteady path home and went to bed.

It was seven in the morning, when Adam woke with a raging thirst and drowsily made his way down to the kitchen, to get a glass of water.

'I hate mornings!' he thought.

At ten past seven, the doorbell rang, which Adam thought was unusual for New Year's Day, but, as there was no one else up, he thought he'd see who it was. Through the frosted glass, he could see someone waiting on the step.

'Who is it?' he asked.

'Hello, nephew. You and I have unfinished business,' came the reply.

# Discussion point and writing prompts

- What is the definition of "human trafficking?"

- What factors would cause a person to want to leave his or her family and pay someone to transport them to another country?

- How common is human trafficking in the UK?

- What would you do if you suspected that human trafficking was taking place near you?

- What do you think is the key that Adam takes from Lauren's bedside cabinet?

- Plan and write an alternative ending to the novel.

- Plan and write a review of the novel.

# Acknowledgements

I wish that the subject matter in this novel was just fiction and that human trafficking and modern slavery didn't exist, but they do, and they are taking place right now all over the world. I dread to think how many real 'Helias' there are. I hope that, in a small way, this story will draw some attention to all the victims and to those who are trying to free them.

This novel would not exist without my friend and former colleague, Vanessa Ward, who gave me the original idea and encouraged me to 'have a go' and try to make something out of it. Her ideas and imagination, led to so many of the important 'moments' in the narrative and she deserves to be recognised as playing a fundamental role in the creation of this story. She is in reality a co-author.

I am also deeply indebted to my friend of almost fifty-years, Mark Eklid, who helped me to shape the narrative and who patiently guided me through the process of getting this novel published, while at the same time developing his own burgeoning career as an author.

Special thanks must go to my publisher, Steven Kay, for being so calm and patient, throughout.

Finally and most importantly, I must thank Susan, James and Liam, for their patience, over the last few years. Watching me do anything is never a pretty sight!